The Art of Reinvention

BOBBE TATREAU

iUniverse®

THE ART OF REINVENTION

iUniverse books may be ordered through booksellers or by contacting:

iUniverse
1663 Liberty Drive
Bloomington, IN 47403
www.iuniverse.com
844-349-9409

ISBN: 978-1-6632-3704-0 (sc)
ISBN: 978-1-6632-3705-7 (e)

Library of Congress Control Number: 2022905302

Print information available on the last page.

iUniverse rev. date: 03/29/2022

CNN: Breaking News

"We have just learned that the tour bus carrying the Grammy Award winning band *Gaining Ground* crashed tonight on the autostrada south of Florence, Italy, killing lead singer/guitarist Jay Mercury and injuring eleven other passengers who have been taken to local area hospitals. Their conditions are unknown."

Because Sophia Perillo had a late afternoon rehearsal in Denver with the Colorado Symphony, she didn't learn about the accident until she walked into her house in Evergreen just after 7 o'clock. Her nine-year old daughter Holly was in tears.

"Aunt Mikki's been in an accident and Jay's dead. Grampa saw it on the news and called. He said you weren't answering your cell." Holly stopped to take a breath. "You shouldn't turn off your phone. What if I got kidnapped?"

Ignoring Holly's reprimand, Sophia sank onto the couch in front of the TV and turned on CNN. When the story recycled a few minutes later, the announcer didn't add anything new to Holly's report. Understandable, since it was just after 4 a.m. in Italy. Most of that country was asleep.

Heart racing, throat tight, Sophia dug her cell out of her purse, first checking her texts, then scrolling to her father's number in Greeley.

He answered immediately. "Do you know anything?" She could hear the worry in his voice.

"No. I just got home. Mikki has both of us listed as next of kin so, since we haven't been contacted, that might be good news." She was trying to be positive for her father and Holly. "But then she might have lost her phone and ID." *So much for being positive.* "I'll try the band's office in Chicago and call you as soon as I find out anything."

In spite of all the technological wonders of the twenty-first century, Sophia couldn't get answers. *Gaining Ground's* phone number went straight to voicemail, and its elaborate website was temporarily off line, probably sinking under the weight of families and fans trying to learn the fate of the other band members and the support crew that made the international performances possible.

If Mikki had access to a phone, she would surely call. Because she hadn't, a tangible dread crept over Sophia.

Holly's arms were crossed tightly against her stomach—her *I'm scared* pose. Sophia reached out and pulled her daughter in against her. "Where's your dad?"

A quavering answer, "He's delivering the coffee table to Mr. Prescott. S'posed to be back in time for dinner."

"Did you call him?"

Holly shook her head.

Sophia tried Dante's cell, but didn't even get voicemail. Prescott's ranch probably didn't have good satellite coverage. She was too upset about her sister to be upset that Dante had left Holly alone—again. One upset at a time.

It was Holly who suggested going on Facebook and Twitter to see whether social media had picked up the story, but only the death of Jay Mercury was getting any coverage.

No additional information came until the next morning when Sophia had a text message from the *Gaining Ground* office: **Mikki is in Santa Maria Nuova Hospital in Florence, recovering from emergency surgery on her left hand. She's stable. Teri Osborne, Business Manager**. Included was the hospital's phone number.

When Sophia checked with her father, she learned he'd received the same message but had no luck getting past the gatekeepers at the Italian hospital. Not speaking Italian was part of the problem; a poor overseas connection contributed.

Mikki Richards was crawling through the fog pressing against her, puzzling over the smells assaulting her—none of them pleasant—and a babble of voices she couldn't understand. Maybe speaking Italian. Instead of trying to decode what they were saying, she relaxed into the foglike cushion surrounding her and went to sleep.

The next time she encountered the fog, it came with a detailed replay of the crash—the tour bus skidding on the rain-slick road, the rear end fishtailing, somebody screaming as the bus slid off the pavement into a field. She'd been asleep in the back, curled across two seats. Without a seat belt to hold her down, she'd been smacked against the window, her left hand trapped between the metal frame of the seat in front of her and the side of the bus. Lightning pain raced up her arm. When she could no longer bear it, she blacked out.

Two days after the accident, Sophia finally received a text from Mikki: **Yes, I'm alive, barely. I'm being sent to some sort of rehab. Don't know when I can leave Italy. M.** Short and lacking in detail. Mikki was never good at communicating with her family.

The trip from Florence to Denver took twelve plus hours, in addition to the two hour layover in London. All of the flying was during daylight, making sleep difficult even with the window shades down and the cabin lights dimmed. Of course being squashed into Economy didn't help. With Teri's contacts, Mikki had, at the last minute, been able to get an aisle seat in a bulkhead row since she was going to need assistance during the flight.

It had been almost a year since she had flown to Europe with *Gaining Ground*. Because Jay's band had been at the top of its game, they flew First Class. Plenty of liquor, decent food, and no crying children.

Today, managing even the small roll-on bag was tricky since her left arm was in a sling, her hand and forearm in a cast that left just the tips of her fingers visible. The flight attendant lifted Mikki's roll-on into the overhead bin for her, held her purse while she sat down, then fastened her seatbelt. So many simple jobs required two hands. Once she was settled, she slipped her arm out of the sling. Her neck was beginning to ache.

Because her Chicago condo was leased until early June, she would be staying with Sophia in Evergreen, an hour's drive west of Denver. Jay's European tour was originally scheduled to end the first week of May. Afterward, she'd planned on visiting a college friend who lived in Lucerne, then doing some sightseeing on her own. *Gaining Ground* didn't have any new projects scheduled until fall. During their time in Europe, Jay had been preparing material for a new album—the first in two years. But that, and so many other things, would never happen. Because he'd been the driving force and the over-the-top talent that fueled their success, his death meant the end of *Gaining Ground*.

Her career wiped out in an instant.

Being unemployed was only one of Mikki's problems. A pianist, especially a jazz pianist, needed two functioning hands. The result of the repair work the Italian surgeon had done on her smashed hand wouldn't be known until the cast came off. Maybe more surgery would be necessary, extensive physical therapy certainly. Mikki had the name of the Denver doctor who had already received her medical files from Florence. Whether she'd ever play as well as she had or play at all, she had no idea. The demons that wanted to tell her that her career was over just wouldn't shut up. When she was Holly's age, jazz became her passion, was still her passion. She didn't know how to do anything else. She **did not want** to do anything else.

When Mikki walked into the Arrivals area at DIA, Holly spotted her first, "Hey, Aunt Mikki!" It had been nearly two years since Mikki had seen her niece, who was running toward her. Holly was tall for her age, a younger version of her mother but with her father's lush dark hair. Fortunately, Holly stopped just before giving her aunt a hug. "Will I hurt you?"

Probably.

"How about a kiss instead?"

Holly complied and took the roll-on's handle from her as they walked toward Sophia. Holly excitedly delivering a monologue about the wonders of the airport.

Only half listening, Mikki was struggling to take in the surreal surroundings. Maybe it was the jet lag or hearing American English all around her, instead of the cacophony of European languages she'd been living with, that was separating her from the scene. She forced herself to focus on Sophia, in designer jeans and a long-sleeved silk blouse, pushing an empty luggage cart and asking something Mikki couldn't quite hear.

Sophia kissed her cheek. "I said, do you have more baggage than that?"

"Oh, sorry. When I finally cleared passport control, I walked right by the carousel. There are two large ones."

With a tinge of older sister exasperation, Sophia handed her purse to Holly. "What do they look like?"

"Bright red, hard sided with mustard-yellow *Gaining Ground* labels." Jay had bought everyone on the tour the same luggage so the support crew could more easily keep track of the hundred plus pieces that traveled with the tour.

Sophia hurried toward the circling carousel.

A pony-tailed teenager looking for his own luggage helped her load Mikki's cases—**Heavy** tags tied to the handles—onto the luggage cart. Getting them into the bed of Dante's pick-up took her and Holly and a kind man who was passing by. Sophia had wanted Dante to come help with the logistics but, as always, there was a rush order he had to finish. At least he offered the use of his pick-up.

As Mikki awkwardly maneuvered herself into the passenger seat, Holly climbed into the extended cab. Sophia slid behind the wheel and caught her breath. "Those suitcases are really heavy. Did you pack rocks?"

"Mostly my performance wardrobe, a few souvenirs."

"It's another hour to my house. Will you be okay?" Sophia fastened her seat belt, then did Mikki's.

"Probably. Too many hours in the air. Do you have a bottle of water? I need to take a pain pill."

From the back, Holly reached between the front seats, "Here, I took the lid off."

Sophia started the noisy diesel engine and switched on the heater; the spring weather they'd had last week had returned to winter.

For most of the trip through Denver and onto I-70, sweeping up into the Front Range, Mikki dosed, her head resting against the side window, the water bottle still clutched in her right hand. When it was safe to momentarily take her eyes from the Interstate, Sophia stole a quick look at her younger sister. Mikki was paler than typical, her hair in the process of reverting to its natural brown. Mikki had always referred to it as mouse brown, streaking it blonde before she was out of high school. Today, it fell loosely onto her shoulders, the rich brown making her look younger, softer.

While Sophia was relieved Mikki was alive, having her in Evergreen, needing a certain amount of care, was at best inconvenient. As a second violinist with the Colorado Symphony, she was gearing up for the busy summer performance schedule: a long weekend at Red Rocks, numerous concerts in cities along the Front Range, as well as those in Boettcher Concert Hall. And she had recently applied to be the principal second violinist, a job that entailed additional responsibilities and an increase in salary. On the other hand, having Mikki in the house might help with childcare. In June, Holly would be in summer camp for two weeks but, after that, caring for her would be more complicated. Because Dante's jobs weren't predictable, he couldn't be counted on to fill in. It had been simpler when Holly was a baby. Sophia took her to rehearsals, grateful she was a good sleeper. In those days, she and Dante were still living in Denver. No hour-long commute each way for Sophia, but not enough space for Dante to expand his furniture business. By the time Holly was ready for kindergarten, they'd saved enough to qualify for a loan and build a house on the land Dante's grandfather had left him. The next year, they built the workshop/office.

Mikki woke when Sophia stopped in the wide driveway that divided the workshop from the house. She straightened herself and studied the house through the windshield, a sprawling brown-brick ranch style. If Mikki remembered correctly, Holly's room and the guest room were in one wing, the master bedroom and Sophia's soundproof practice studio in the other. The last time she'd visited was when the band performed at Red Rocks two years ago.

This wasn't exactly a visit—more a rescue. She had nowhere else to go right now. Their father and his girlfriend Ardith lived in her house in Greeley. Mikki hadn't felt comfortable asking. She hardly knew Ardith. Sophia had physical room for her but, given her busy lifestyle, a damaged, temporarily condo-less and unemployed sister wasn't on her agenda.

Hopefully, the band had continued paying her. She needed to get her head around practical matters.

Just not right now.

The day Mikki's cast was scheduled to come off coincided with one of Sophia's Saturday morning rehearsals at Boettcher Hall, so Mikki and Holly rode into Denver with her. Armed with a library book, Holly stayed in the rehearsal hall while Mikki carefully drove herself to the medical center. She was able to use her left arm to help with driving, but she was nervous because she couldn't grasp the steering wheel with both hands. Sophia had spent several hours riding around Evergreen with her sister, making sure she could safely drive to the appointment. After all, it was Sophia's car.

Mikki didn't really want anyone with her for this medical evaluation. Whether the news was good or bad, she preferred to face it by herself, pretty much the way she'd faced almost everything else since she left the university and joined Jay's fledgling band nearly seven years ago.

She heard about Jay Mercury's talent before she met him. The Northwestern School of Music grapevine had quickly picked up on his triad of skills—vocal, acoustic guitar, and composing. In the Fall quarter, Jay, Mikki, and bass player Noah Stein were enrolled in the Thursday night Small Jazz Ensemble, 6 to 9 p.m. Noah and Mikki were seniors, Jay a junior. She'd rather imagined Jay would be tall and lanky with unkempt, shoulder length hair. Instead, he was built more like an NFL lineman, dishwater blond hair curling at the top of his ears, his fair skin easily sunburned after ten minutes outside. Surprisingly, he didn't have the world-weary demeanor some musicians cultivated. He had a mischievous smile and was easy to like.

During that Fall quarter, Jay was performing Friday-Saturday-Sunday nights at The Rooftop, a high-end restaurant and night club on the North Shore. The weekend before Thanksgiving, he was *discovered* when a well-known food critic devoted half of his Rooftop critique to Jay's music, and he was suddenly being offered gigs all over Chicago. Understandably, he didn't return for the Winter quarter. Once he explained to Mikki and Noah that he wanted them to be part of his new band, they followed him.

Mikki's father was horrified. "You'll graduate in June. You need to finish." Though she only needed four units to complete her degree, Mikki wasn't interested in being practical. Having been force-fed classical music by her late mother and various piano teachers, she had rebelled during middle school and switched to jazz. Because she loved improvising, Jay's music—a blend of blues, soul, pop and jazz—suited her. The opportunity to be part of *Gaining Ground* was too good to pass up.

Three years before, Sophia had sensibly graduated from Northwestern, was gradually working her way into the classical world, and had recently gotten engaged to Dante. The conventional daughter. In contrast, Mikki and the band members were often on the road, living out of suitcases, catching red-eye flights, drinking more than they should. Nothing conventional about Mikki's gypsy lifestyle. She loved it, expected it would last forever.

Based on the restaurant review, New York venues sent out feelers, though Jay didn't succumb to the job offers immediately. He was waiting until his band, now composed of Mikki, Noah, drummer Buddy Kim, and electric guitarist Earle Savage, was ready. No sense racing into a larger limelight and then failing. The same month that Mikki would have graduated, the band debuted at The Rooftop to rave reviews. A year later, their popularity in the Midwest firmly established, they took on New York. The next year, they were dazzling the West Coast, their first album winning a Grammy.

Gaining Ground had hit the big time.

The band spent much of its fifth year in a Chicago recording studio, working on their second album, glad to be in one place for more than a few weeks at a time. That was the year Mikki's father pressured her into using some of the money she was making to invest in a piece of real estate. He even stooped to the *for a rainy day* argument, pointing out that the music business could be fickle.

She laughed at the cliché. "Like I don't know that!"

"Just saying. Remember, I teach Economics so I know about finance." Mikki didn't remind him that university professors didn't earn all that much money. His investments were few and far between.

She was still laughing when she hung up. She did however recognize he was right. She had been sharing Teri's condo while the band was working on the new album but really needed a place of her own. Six months before Jay put together the European tour, she bought a one-bedroom condo in a high rise two blocks from Lake Michigan. The condo was still not completely furnished when she asked the building's property manager to find someone to lease it while she was, once again, on the move.

By the time Mikki returned to Boettcher Hall, her brain was suspended somewhere between hope and fear, grateful that Sophia took over the driving. Her left arm was aching. After a seemingly endless number of X-rays, the doctor was satisfied that the bones in Mikki's hand had healed and was hopeful there would be no need for more surgery, despite the hand being weak and sort of shrunken. With very little flexibility and a web of red lines that would be permanent scars, it was hard to imagine it belonged to her. In place of the cast, she was now wearing a lightweight, removable brace that left her fingers free but supported her wrist and palm. No lifting or pulling. And no touching the piano. In the weeks to come, she would be facing the reality of whether her hand would regain the strength and agility needed to play jazz—or anything.

Immediately after the crash, she had been numb, grieving Jay's death and the death of the band. Grappling with anger about what had been snatched from all of them so quickly. The others would find new groups, but she was afraid she had no musical future. The doctor's evaluation hadn't been negative but it wasn't positive either.

Over lunch in a booth at Panera—Sophia's preference, Holly had pleaded for KFC—Mikki gave them the abridged version of her morning. Finishing with "Fortunately Dr. Conroy chose a physical therapist in a clinic in Evergreen instead of Denver. I have my first appointment next Wednesday morning."

"How long will the therapy take?" Because Holly would soon be out of school, Sophia was rather hoping it might last through summer.

"No idea. I can't touch the piano." She sighed, "Dr. Conroy said she'll keep in touch with the therapist, Hank Duncan."

Holly turned to Mikki, "That's Erin's father. She's in my class."

Sophia pushed aside her empty salad bowl and reached for her half sandwich. She was always starving after a rehearsal, "Is he the one who's a single dad?"

Her mouth full, Holly could only nod.

Though the shock of Jay's death was lessening, Mikki felt she had been dropped into a foreign land. People got up before ten o'clock and went to bed before midnight. Her body clock was struggling to recalibrate itself. Without her music, she was adrift. Nothing to replace it in the short or long term. She'd never done much cooking, so she wasn't any help in Sophia's kitchen. Holly knew more than she did. She offered to help Dante in his office, but he already had a part-time assistant. So she and Holly spent time together, playing games, going for walks.

Because she needed transportation of her own, Dante called a friend at a Ford agency in Denver. A few days later, Mikki bought a three-year old, white Ford Escape. It had been a long time since she'd had a car of her own, but she couldn't continue borrowing Sophia's car to go to appointments.

Teri Osborne had been regularly emailing Mikki about the plans for Jay's Celebration of Life in Kankakee, south of Chicago. His family still lived there. Mikki was dreading reconnecting with the other band members, having to revisit the details of the crash, share memories about Jay. And she didn't want to talk about her damaged hand. She'd had two emails from Noah—which she hadn't answered. He had an offer from a New Orleans band and was moving on. She wanted to be happy for him, but the rock of self-pity that was sitting on her heart interfered. After two months in limbo, she was afraid she might end up teaching. Those who can do, those who can't—

While she was in Chicago, she needed to talk to the property management company about her condo. Should she sell or lease it again? At this point, she couldn't imagine moving back to Chicago. Since she'd only owned the unit for two years, there probably wasn't much equity in it. She was fairly sure her father would tell her to keep it for a rainy day, but Mikki was pretty sure the rain was already falling.

When she'd asked her sister whether she could stay with her once she left Italy, Sophia hadn't hesitated. "Of course, of course." She'd been so thankful that Mikki was alive, she'd have agreed to anything and, fortunately, Mikki didn't require much care, keeping to herself most of the time, contributing financially to the household expenses. Just two trips to Denver and one visit from their father on a Sunday afternoon.

The first word that came to mind when Jon Richards saw Mikki standing on Sophia's front porch was *fragile*. He could tell that his younger daughter was not the confident—I can do anything I set my mind to—person she'd always been. And she no longer had blonde streaks. He'd almost forgotten what her real hair color was. She didn't go to greet him, waiting until he was on the porch—then letting him pull her into a bear hug. "Welcome home, sweetheart. Sorry to be so long getting up here."

"S'okay." When he released her, he saw tears and wiped at them with his thumb.

"Do you want to sit out here or go inside?"

"Here. When Holly realizes you've arrived, she'll want your undivided attention."

"Tell me about it. The few times she's stayed with Ardith and me for a weekend, I am worn out when she goes home. But since she's my only grandchild——" He enjoyed giving her a hard time about not adding to his pool of grandchildren. Usually she teased back. Not today.

Side-by-side on the swing, both fell silent, not sure what should come next.

To keep the conversation away from the reason she was at Sophia's, Mikki asked, "How's Ardith?" Though Jon and Ardith had begun dating four years ago, Mikki didn't know her well because Mikki was usually somewhere other than Colorado. Ardith was a high school counselor who worked eleven months of the year.

"Busy. The end of the school year gets crazy in high school. Graduation and annuals and seniors ditching class."

More silence.

Finally, he ventured, "How are you?"

Mikki shrugged. If she answered, her voice would give her away. It was one thing to maintain a stiff upper lip with her sister, quite another to try that with her father, who would see right through her. He'd always been able to read her moods.

His steady gaze told her he knew. "That bad?"

"Yeah." Carefully she undid the Velcro on the brace. Might as well let him look at her hand, see the scar.

He laid her hand on his palm. "Are you on pain meds?"

"As needed. I have my first PT appointment Wednesday. It's probably not going to be fun."

"What's the prognosis?"

Another shrug. "Just that I should be patient."

He grinned. "Not your best quality."

Reluctantly she found a smile. "True."

"Will you stay here or find another place?"

"Don't know. With Holly out of school, I suspect Soph would like me to stay. The symphony has a busy summer schedule, and Dante isn't always available." She slid her hand off her father's comforting palm and refastened the brace. "I'm thinking of selling my condo." When he didn't jump in with advice, "There's nothing for me in Chicago and, though there are still royalties coming in for the albums, I'm essentially unemployed."

"Any idea what the condo's worth?"

"No. It's in a good location." She'd been trying to hide from the decision waiting in Chicago. Selling the condo would be admitting that chapter of her life was done. No encores. At the moment, her focus was on her hand and whether therapy would give it back to her. Without the ability to play, her professional life was over. No matter how often she reminded herself it had only been nine weeks since the surgery, she kept dragging her despair around behind her. Even afraid to practice scales with her right hand.

Jon was actually grateful when Holly found them. He'd run out of things to talk about, and Mikki wasn't much help. Holly being Holly happily filled the uncomfortable distance. He'd brought his granddaughter two of the Nancy Drew books she hadn't read. They might be a bit ahead of her age level, but she was a voracious reader and books designated for her age seemed too bland.

In between squeals of pleasure: "How did you know which ones I haven't read?"

"Ardith has been keeping track."

Holly turned the pages, not reading yet, savoring the pleasure of a new book she knew she would love. Thank you." She hugged him.

When Sophia finished practicing, she stopped in the kitchen before joining her family on the porch. She took the pitcher of lemonade she'd made that morning out of the fridge and removed the foil from a platter of cookies—Pepperidge Farm, not homemade. Holly had set the books on the porch floor and was telling her grandfather about her summer camp which would begin in two weeks. As Sophia set the lemonade on the low table, Holly jumped up, "Can I pour it?"

"Yes. Bring the glasses that are on the kitchen table. I didn't have enough hands." She leaned down to kiss her father's cheek and settled herself in the chair across from him.

"How long can you stay?"

Jon glanced at his watch, "I need to leave around four. Ardith's parents are coming for dinner. What are you practicing?"

"Shoshtakovich."

He chuckled. "I shouldn't ask. I almost never know who the classical composers are. Your mother was the expert on all things classical. Mikki's music is more to my taste."

"Dante's too. And that's why the studio is soundproof."

"Where is Dante?"

"He and Sergio are at the handmade furniture showcase in the Springs, scouting for new customers. They'll be back tomorrow."

"No wives allowed?"

"I used to go, but—" she didn't finish the thought. Holly was carefully pouring the lemonade and passing glasses around.

Jon raised his glass: "I haven't had my three girls together in a long time. Cheers."

He studied them: Holly so full of herself, excited about the world. Mikki, who had always run toward every challenge, wasn't herself yet, and Sophia, who appeared to have things under control, might not. It occurred to him that he rarely saw Dante these days, as though he and Sophia were functioning in different time zones. He liked Dante, though he had to admit he didn't know him all that well. Initially, he'd been concerned that Dante and Sophia had very different backgrounds and talents. Dante, a master craftsman running a business. Sophia surrounded by her music, coping with the demands of the orchestra, as well as Holly and the house.

He looked away from whatever problems there might be on that front. Worrying about Mikki was more urgent.

Hank Duncan's weekdays began at 5 a.m. After his run, he put in a load of laundry—there was always laundry—and made sure Erin and Cate were awake. After his shower, he checked that the girls were really moving, then set out a variety of cereal boxes, fruit, and lunch possibilities because he never correctly guessed what they wanted to eat. Supplying a do-it-yourself kitchen was easier than listening to their complaints. Cate had to be at the corner by 7:30 for the high school bus. She refused to let Hank drive her to the campus—too embarrassing. Erin was still more than happy to be dropped off at the elementary school. Fathers were less embarrassing when you were ten.

He arrived at the Mountaintop Clinic a little after eight. Besides Hank, the clinic had a GP, a Pediatrician, and an Allergist. Receptionist Betty Jamison was already opening mail and had made the first of many pots of coffee. He picked up his messages and clipboard with the day's schedule. Everyone else on the staff kept their schedules on their phones or tablets, but he liked having something he could write on during an appointment.

Seven years ago, Hank was beginning a residency in orthopedic surgery when his wife Taylor decided marriage and motherhood were interfering with her career prospects and accepted a high profile job in New York's financial district. Then she filed for divorce. Goodbye residency. Eventually, he was able to cobble together the requirements to obtain a Physical Therapist's license. Working at the clinic was a better fit for raising the girls. He kept regular hours and his mother lived nearby.

Grace Duncan delivered casseroles, babysat when necessary, taught him how to braid their hair, and took her granddaughters shopping for clothes. She willingly handled the birds and bees discussion with Cate and promised to do the same with Erin.

The effects of Taylor's abrupt exit lingered at the edge of their lives. The girls texted her, talked to her on Facetime, spent a week with her in the summer, once going to Disneyworld, once to Hawaii. Several times, she flew to Denver for a few days between Christmas and New Years. But nothing could make up for the absence of day-to-day mothering. Even Taylor's distracted mothering. And now she was reportedly engaged to some big-name actor. Cate, at least, was quite impressed, hoping for an invitation to the New York wedding. Hank was not impressed.

After Erin's birth, he'd foolishly ignored the signs that his wife was restless and had her sights set on more than being a wife and mother. When Cate was a baby, Taylor took her to the child-care center provided by the brokerage house. But four years later, when Erin was born, balancing a job and family life got harder. When she made vice-president and was soon offered a position at the New York headquarters, he assumed she'd turn the transfer down. Instead, she'd been quick to remind him of the sacrifices she'd made to support him as he made his way through medical school. Now it was her turn.

End of discussion.

Because they agreed not to uproot the girls or shuttle them between two households, he obtained full custody; she had visitation rights and paid child support.

Hank's first patient this morning was Steve Garcia, a sixteen-year old skier who had underestimated the difficulty of a run at Breckenridge and had done major damage to his right knee. Steve's primary concern was being ready to ski this winter. The second patient was new, Mikki Richards, a pianist sidelined by a bus crash. He'd seldom had a patient with a hand injury as severe as hers, so he'd spent additional time studying the medical records and X-rays Dr. Conroy had forwarded to him.

She arrived early. Attractive, but not conventionally pretty, wide set eyes, brown hair. No smile. During her appointment, Hank focused on assessing her range of motion. Half an hour into the appointment, he was fairly sure she was going to be difficult to rein in. He began with some basic movements, testing for flexibility, then evaluated her strength. She went after each task intensely, as though she had to prove—right now— how much she could do.

"Not so hard. You need to start easy, build a little at a time."

She stopped squeezing the soft rubber ball he'd given her.

"Don't get ahead of yourself or healing will actually take longer."

Instantly defensive, "I need my hand back."

"Of course you do. But not all at once."

She drew her lips tightly together, perhaps to keep from arguing with him.

He liked her spirit. Spirit was useful in this process. Patients who whined or claimed they couldn't do what he asked before they tried, were only slowing their recovery and, in truth, trying his patience. Her determination was a good sign. He took her left hand, placed it palm down on the small examination table between them and carefully chose his words.

"Your hand will improve. I can promise you that. But I can't promise that it will be as good as it was." When she didn't respond, he tried to draw her out. "I understand you and the band were very good and very famous."

Quietly, "Yes."

"Will the band regroup?"

"Probably not."

He wondered whether she was naturally this quiet or whether the trauma of the accident was muting her. Hard to read. Still nothing resembling a smile. And he suspected it might be a compelling smile to go along with her dark eyes and good cheekbones. He quickly reminded himself that her looks should not be part of his evaluation of her injury. Nevertheless, her eyes followed him around the rest of the day. It had been a while since he found himself attracted to a woman so quickly.

Mikki watched the therapist—Hank—move her hand this way and that, bending her fingers, telling her to stop him when it hurt too much. Measuring her reach from thumb to little finger and the spread between each finger. He had her press each finger on some sort of electronic strip to determine her strength. How much of a fist she could make. On and on. All of it hurt, some actions more than others. She'd secretly been hoping her hand would miraculously prove to the therapist that she could soon return to playing. Instead, he was holding her back.

She was sent home with diagrams of the exercises he wanted her to do: how many repetitions, how often each day. And an appointment for the following Wednesday.

Because she had been concentrating on her hand, the only thing she could tell Sophia about him was that he had strong hands and a quiet voice. Mikki wasn't sure she'd recognize him if she saw him on the street.

What she was sure of was that her hand ached and she was disappointed.

The morning after the appointment, Mikki opened four emails from Teri Osborne. One containing various legal documents cancelling her contract with the band that was no longer a band, another explaining the way the insurance coverage would be handled because the accident occurred in a foreign country; the third was a financial statement of her earnings, year to date. From this point on, there would only be sporadic royalty payments from the albums. In the last email, Teri asked if Mikki would speak at Jay's memorial service. That one made her cry. She waited a few days before accepting. Speaking in front of large groups had never been her thing. She preferred letting music talk for her.

Maybe Noah and I can do something together.

Every time she tried to figure out what she might say, her mind wandered to their final performance in Rome at the Parco della Musica, an elaborate outdoor arena that held nearly three thousand fans. For two and a half hours, *Gaining Ground* gave Rome their best. Colored lights playing against the night sky, Jay in superb form, her two solos, new compositions Jay had written during their time in Europe. Nothing quite like the swelling applause from an audience to push her to play better than she thought she could. The magnetic connection between the performers and the crowd kept the adrenaline high. At the end of the concert, thousands of multi-colored balloons were released into the night. No one expected this was the band's final performance.

In so many ways, performing with *Gaining Ground* had been a larger than life experience. She went from being a student to being in a hugely popular band, being catapulted into a much wider world than her childhood in Colorado. The band worked hard, yet the resulting fame felt effortless; sometimes she worried that it had come too easily. Though most of the attention was trained on Jay, the rest of the band enjoyed the benefits of his charisma, signing autographs for fans and snapping selfies with them.

Mikki had a Facebook page but wasn't faithful about posting information about herself. She was uncomfortable with that kind of sharing. Since the crash, she hadn't looked at any of the *Gaining Ground* sites. Didn't want to know what was being posted. Hiding. And no, she didn't want to talk to a shrink—Sophia's suggestion—about her grief. The only thing that was important right now was healing her hand.

Losing Jay and the band was like losing brothers, though Noah had been more than a brother their junior year at Northwestern. By the time Jay was forming the band, she and Noah had moved on to other partners.

Most romantic relationships were complicated at one time or another but, for Mikki, her commitment to the band and her music made any serious relationship close to impossible. Traveling, rehearsing, performing. Hooking up with someone in the band or in the support staff was a definite no-no. If the affair went south, all sorts of relationships would be out of whack. Her only recent, semi-serious affair occurred when the band was working on the album in Chicago. Jack Simmons, the real estate agent who sold her the condo, was recently divorced and not looking for anything permanent. Mikki wasn't either. Their break up was more a drifting apart. Being part of *Gaining Ground* was more important. And in the last year, she'd begun composing again, asking Jay to give her feedback. To encourage her, he'd put one of her shorter pieces on the program during their performance in London.

She'd always seen Sophia's career decision as safe, though playing in a major orchestra was no small thing; auditions for those jobs were highly competitive, paying just half what she would have earned in New York or Chicago. There was only a modest amount of traveling, not enough to interfere with having a family. However, since Mikki'd been staying with the Perillos, she sensed that safe didn't mean easy. Managing two careers had initially been doable, but Holly's arrival made their lives more complicated.

Dante—olive skinned, dark haired, and perhaps too handsome—was a workaholic. He had a part time assistant, Louise, who handled the paperwork, ran errands, and occasionally cleaned the office inside the workshop. She had two teenage sons playing high school soccer and a firefighter husband. Besides Louise, there was a young apprentice, Sergio, who couldn't decide what he wanted to do with his life. His best friend wanted him to join the Marines with him, his parents wanted him to go to the local community college, but Sergio wanted to work with his hands. So far, Dante had him doing a lot of the tedious work: sanding, applying finishes, and cleaning up the workshop. Dante preferred making the designs, working with customers, and shopping for the wood. Turning beautiful wood into unique pieces of furniture was as much an addiction for him as music was for Sophia and Mikki. Unlike his schedule, Sophia's was somewhat predictable: what Holly needed and what the orchestra required. When Holly was out of school, Sophia needed Dante to be home when the symphony had a rehearsal or performance. Sometimes he was, but not always. Her resentment had been festering too long.

Mikki was at sixes and sevens with herself. No immediate purpose, nothing to do but exercise her hand, watch out for Holly, and wait for the memorial service. The payoff for all the exercising was that Hank Duncan had become quietly approving of her progress, though she couldn't see enough improvement.

Hank was still adamant about her staying away from the piano.

"But—"

He cut her off. "Maybe gentle practice in two weeks or so."

"By then, I'll be in Chicago."

"Because?"

"The memorial service for Jay Mercury."

A slight frown, "I don't know who that is."

Which planet did he live on? "The leader of the band I—the leader of *Gaining Ground*. He died in the crash that did this to my hand."

"Oh—sorry." He smiled—it was an engaging smile that unfolded in stages. "My daughters tell me I don't get out enough. My older girl, Cate, probably knows about *Gaining Ground*."

"The service is south of Chicago at his parents' church in Kankakee."

"Will it be a huge affair?"

"Medium. He was well-respected in the musical world. There'll probably be fans clamoring to attend, but it's by invitation only. The church is small."

Hank rolled his chair back a little and studied her. "If I looked you up online, would I find that you are also well-known in the music world?"

"Since I was part of the band, I suppose I'm mentioned someplace." She actually hadn't looked in a long time.

"So no agent or entourage?" She realized he was teasing, not something he'd done before. She liked it.

"No. I left that to Jay. However, I do have a skype appointment to talk to a reporter from the *Chicago Tribune* tomorrow. The paper is doing a spread on Jay to run the day of the memorial. I understand all the band members and the support staff have been contacted." In the past, the band members did things like this together, but they were in different parts of the country now.

"Were they injured too?"

She glanced down at her hand, "Jay and —well, a few others." She took a deep breath to steady herself. "Jay was standing in the aisle talking to our stage manager when the crash happened. He was thrown the length of the bus, hitting his head on the metal equipment boxes stored in the back of the bus." She stopped. She hadn't even explained that to Sophia. Her voice wavered. "He died instantly."

"Where were you?"

"Toward the back, asleep. I grabbed for the railing on the seat in front of me just about the time that seat was smashed into the side of the bus."

He reached into the paper sleeve holding her X-rays, pulled one out, and held it to the light for a moment. "That explains what the first Italian X-rays show." He slid it back into the sleeve but didn't elaborate. He stood up, all business, no more teasing. "My next appointment is due. See you next week."

The Thursday afternoon before her Friday flight to Chicago, Mikki dropped Holly off at Grace Duncan's house for Erin's tenth birthday party. Grace had a backyard pool, so no organized entertainment was necessary. Two hours later, when Mikki returned, Holly was watching for her. "Mrs. Duncan says to have a piece of birthday cake."

Mikki reluctantly followed her niece around the side of the house, a modest 1950's frame structure with a wide lawn and two greenhouses along the back boundary. In her best managing style, Holly instructed her to sit at the end of the extra-long picnic table bench and brought her a piece of carrot cake. "You'll love it." She raced off.

It took Mikki a few minutes to realize that the man sitting next to her, talking to a teenage girl on his other side, was her therapist. When he finished his conversation, he turned to her in surprise. "Did you just arrive?"

"I came to pick up Holly and have been ordered to eat cake. Why are you here?"

Until now, she'd only seen him wearing a white lab coat over slacks and usually a polo shirt. Now he was in cargo Bermudas and a light green t-shirt.

"Erin's my daughter. Fathers are required to show up for cake and presents. And to supervise what's going on in the pool. I took the afternoon off."

"Oh, right. I guess I forgot." Somehow she hadn't put the pieces together. The teenage girl he'd been talking to must be his older daughter. "And Holly is?"

"My sister's daughter. Sophia's at a rehearsal in Denver. This weekend is the beginning of the summer season for the Symphony performances. Friday, Saturday and Sunday evenings. Bad timing that I'm leaving tomorrow and won't be back until Tuesday."

"Another musician. Are your parents musicians too?"

"Just my mom and not exactly on a professional level. Mostly she was an accompanist for choirs or sometimes schools that were putting on a musical. And she gave lessons."

That made him smile slightly. "Were you one of her pupils?"

"Sophia was. I started, but I wasn't into classical, which is what my mother wanted me to learn. Lessons were torture for both of us. My father never lets me forgot that my jazz piano lessons cost him more than Sophia's. But eventually, she switched to the violin. My mother failed with both of us." She pointed to the greenhouse, "Do those belong to your mother?"

"Yes. She not only makes great carrot cake, but she also supplies flowers to a couple of the local florists. My older daughter is working for her this summer."

"Is that who was sitting next to you?"

"Cate. She's fifteen and just got her learner's permit."

"Who looks after Erin?"

"My mother, sometimes Cate, but not willingly. Bribery is often required."

"You're lucky. Sophia only has me, temporarily."

"Her father works?"

"On the property. He owns Perillo Woods, but he isn't always available. Holly's still too young to be left on her own."

"Hank," Grace Duncan was standing across the picnic table, "sorry to interrupt but the KP crew awaits your oversight."

"Oops, be right there."

Mikki slid off the bench so he could get out.

"I promised to be on clean up. Have a good trip." And he was gone.

Returning to Chicago was a heavy dose of *deja vu*.

Self-conscious, Mikki felt everyone in the hotel dining room was looking at her left hand. She was struggling to keep it hidden in the folds of the long, gauzy skirt she'd chosen for the band's reunion dinner. A filmy wash of greens and blues, matched with a blue tank top. Dressy and comfortable. Her only jewelry, lightweight silver hoop earrings. She'd let Sophia talk her into cutting her hair to chin length while she was wearing the heavy cast—easier to take care of. Most of her professional career, she'd worn her hair long so she could pull it back or put it up. And her hair hadn't been its natural brown since she was fifteen. She hardly recognized herself.

When she checked into the hotel, she texted Noah, and he responded with **You're my date tonight. I'll be at your door at 5:30.**

Knowing him as well at she did, Mikki figured he'd show up about six o'clock.

He arrived at five after.

Seeing him framed in her hotel doorway brought swift tears—just over six feet tall, red hair, a grin that made women of every age fall all over him.

They hugged, stepped back to study each other, then hugged again. The last time she'd seen him was when he visited her in the Italian hospital the day after her surgery. She'd been fuzzy from the medication. Since he'd been in the front of the bus, his injuries were superficial, though he had to stay in Florence a few days until the Italian authorities investigated the accident and talked to all the victims. Then he flew back to Chicago.

"I like the haircut, but I prefer you with the blonde streaky stuff."

"Lots of things have changed." *Perhaps too cryptic.*

"Let's go. We don't want to be late for cocktail hour. Open bar." Again his grin.

One of the best and worst things about Noah was his ability to sidestep difficult topics. He didn't ask to see her hand, ask how she was or what she was going to do about what passed for her life. The rest of the evening would probably not be so easy, nor would tomorrow's memorial service when Jay's family, friends and the musical world would crowd into the family's church. Tonight's dinner was only for those who belonged to *Gaining Ground*.

She was grateful Noah was beside her as they entered the elegant dining room on the top floor of the hotel, the floor to ceiling windows looking out on the Chicago skyline. Four round tables, each seating ten in a dining room designed for twice that number. The elaborate bar was doing a brisk business. Everyone knew everyone. Hugs all-round. But no Jay, the person who had held all these people together. Mikki was surprised no one mentioned him, but then she didn't either. Tonight was for catching up with each other. Where they were working—or not yet working, their families, significant others. Tomorrow was for the past, for talking about Jay.

Teri sat on Mikki's left, Noah on her right. Unlike Noah, Teri immediately asked about Mikki's hand. "Can you use it yet?"

To demonstrate, with her left hand Mikki reached for the cloth napkin in her lap and placed it on the table. "Lightweight stuff that doesn't require fine motor skills. Putting straws in drinks but not carrying a mug of coffee. Bottom line—if what I'm doing hurts, I stop doing it." She tried to keep her tone light. No one really needed, or probably wanted, all the details.

"Let me know if there's a problem with the insurance. What about the clinic? Do you have a good therapist?"

A half smile. "He's a borderline tyrant but seems to know what he's doing. If I so much as mention touching the piano, I'm given to understand that I will do irreparable harm." She paused, never comfortable talking about herself. "What about you? I mean, besides having to put *Gaining Ground* out of business."

"Vince moved in with me." The drummer Teri had been dating when Mikki was staying with her. Two plus years ago.

"I'm happy for you. Are you happy for you?"

Teri shrugged. "So far. But he's a drummer."

Mikki could fill in the blanks. Musicians were a different breed. She should know.

Appropriately, it drizzled all the way to Kankakee. The service was scheduled for 2 p.m., followed by a potluck reception hosted by Jay's family in the church basement. Couldn't get more Midwest than that.

During the drive, Noah and Mikki sketched out what each would say when it was their turn to speak. Because Mikki's all-purpose black sheath didn't have pockets, she'd stuffed Noah's pockets with emergency tissues. She wasn't given to public crying, but talking about Jay could prove dangerous.

At the church parking lot, one of the ushers was saving spots for the band members; otherwise, Noah would have had to hunt for a spot on the surrounding streets. Along the sidewalk in front of the church entrance, behind a band of yellow police tape, a solemn crowd had gathered, smart phones ready to catch shots of celebrities.

The church wasn't large, brownish brick with stained glass windows on each side and a central spire over the double-wide front door. On one side of the main door was an oversized poster of Jay with his guitar, taken during the Rome performance. On the other side, a plain white board with a black border: **Memorial for Jay Allen Mercury: 2 p.m. Invitation Only**

Inside, Mikki signed the guest book for herself and Noah, took two programs and followed the nervous teenage usher, his hair plastered down, wearing a dark suit that looked brand new. Clearly, he had been lectured on doing all the correct things and was careful to ask Noah and Mikki's names before leading them to their seats in the second row alongside Teri. Flowers blanketed the altar. There was no casket because the difficulties of shipping a body from Italy to Illinois had necessitated cremation. Jay hadn't left any instructions about his funeral—no 30 year old did that—but once the band began making money, Teri had badgered him until he made a will. However, without a living trust, Jay's estate would spend a lot of time and money going through probate.

The Minister stepped to the podium a few minutes after two o'clock and spoke about Jay, story after story from when Jay and his two brothers had been in the church Sunday School. His brothers spoke briefly, but his parents had begged off. The band members came last.

Once Noah and Mikki were behind the podium, they held hands for support.

"Hi. I'm Noah Stein, I play double bass. Mikki and I met Jay at Northwestern. He was a huge talent, far beyond any of the rest of us enrolled in the Thursday night, Small Jazz Ensemble class. Fortunately, performance classes aren't graded on a curve because with him in class, I'd have been getting a C. The thing about Jay was that he knew he was good, very, very good—but he had a kind of aww-shucks way about him that let us love him even when we were sometimes intimidated by his talent. He set high standards for *Gaining Ground*, even higher ones for himself." Noah paused. **"Performing with Jay made me a better musician because I didn't want to disappoint him. Knowing him, being in on the beginning of *Gaining Ground* was a gift that can't be matched."**

He squeezed Mikki's right hand, signaling it was her turn. She took a breath.

"Jay"—she cleared her throat—**"Jay was a generous musician. He gave all of us opportunities to show-off. It wasn't all about him. While we were in Europe,"** she paused, waiting for her voice to steady, **"he composed a piece featuring the piano, named it 'Mikki's Song' and let me perform it in Rome..."** her voice vanished.

Noah waited.

"He was special. I miss him."

Her tears won. As they left the podium, Noah handed her the wad of tissues.

Driving back to Chicago, they were silent. Mikki didn't want to revisit the details of the service, the reception, or meeting his grieving family. Memories insisted on pummeling her in spite of her efforts to hide from them. By the way Noah was gripping the steering wheel, she was pretty sure he was processing the day too. She tried closing her eyes, coaxing sleep, but it was impossible to turn her brain off.

Tomorrow, she had an appointment with the manager of the condo complex. She'd brought all the relevant documents so the condo could be sold without her being in Chicago. She'd have to sign a Power of Attorney, make decisions she hadn't planned on before she left for Europe. Most of her personal possessions were already in storage, so she'd have to make arrangements to add the furniture. The piano had been returned to the leasing agency before she left on the tour.

When she was done with that major piece of business, she would have to sort out bank accounts and get everything transferred to Denver for the time being.

As they were leaving the reception in Kankakee, the band members agreed to meet at the English-themed pub across the street from the Chicago hotel at ten o'clock. The solemnity of the day had taken a toll on all of them. They needed the release that playing music could provide. An extemporaneous jam session in honor of Jay.

The pub crowd grew gradually and soon there was standing room only. Word of the jam session had spread. Mikki changed out of the black dress she'd worn all day into jeans and a dressy yellow t-shirt with "Make Music" embroidered on the front. Noah had bought it for her when they were in London.

Alongside the Pub's tiny stage, Mikki was sitting at the upright piano, hands in her lap. She hadn't touched the keys, simply enjoying what remained of *Gaining Ground*. Instead of playing his electric guitar, Earle was on acoustic. Not as flamboyant as Jay, but no one cared. Because Mikki knew all the music inside and out, her body was instinctively keeping time to the music. At the end of each piece, the crowd yelled and clapped and ordered more beer.

An hour into the performance, Mikki lightly brushed the piano keys with her right hand, tempted to join in, not sure whether she could play just the treble clef. She'd always felt as though her hands moved together in a symbiotic memory. When she could no longer resist, she carefully placed both hands on the keys—their cool smoothness telling her she'd come home.

The guys were playing a syncopated arrangement of *Autumn Leaves*. She tried a couple of measures, gradually catching up with their rhythm. No problem with the right hand but she was having to skip some of the complicated chords with the left. It wasn't perfect, but it was playing. She played the next selection. Another. And another.

Suddenly, a piercing pain sliced across her knuckles and her damaged hand froze in a paralyzing spasm. Her right hand grabbed the left, massaging, trying to loosen the muscles.

When Noah realized she was in trouble, he propped his bass against the wall and sat beside her, "What do you need? Ice or heat?"

"Don't know. The brace and pain pills are in my room. Can you come with me?"

They decided on ice once the cramp eased and her hand began to swell. She swallowed one of the pills, sent Noah back to join the jam session, and crawled into bed, trying not to imagine what Hank Duncan would say at her Wednesday appointment.

By morning, the pain had backed off a little, but her hand was still swollen. Tender to the touch. After her shower, she refastened the brace and hoped for the best.

She met Noah for breakfast in the hotel coffee shop. He was flying to New Orleans in a few hours. "I need to find a place to live."

"Will you be traveling much?"

"Not like before. This group has a permanent venue on Bourbon Street. After this last year, I'm ready to stay in one place."

"Let me know how it's going."

"You too."

They hugged goodbye and got into separate taxis, neither mentioning her hand.

The business of listing her condo took the rest of the morning. Papers to sign for this and that. The manager kept a waiting list of people interested in buying one of the units. "I don't think we'll have trouble selling it. And you might even have a small profit after costs." Some good news at least.

Later, Teri filled her in on the plans to use the recordings from the Rome performance as a basis for a final *Gaining Ground* album. At some point next year, there would be royalties, carved up many ways, of course.

Mikki's Denver flight left half an hour late, putting her into DIA at 6:30 Tuesday night. She bought coffee and a saran-wrapped sandwich on her way out of the airport and picked up her car at the Long Stay lot. Because her hand was still painful, the drive to Evergreen would not be easy.

To let her hand rest, she pulled off I-70 at a rest stop, ate the sandwich and drank the now cold coffee. Arriving in Evergreen last April had felt like a temporary pause. This time, it felt more like a dead end. *Gaining*

Ground was truly finished, buried along with Jay's ashes. She and Noah were on different paths. Earle was staying in Chicago, trying out a single act. Buddy, like her, didn't have immediate plans.

The kitchen lights were on at the Perillos' when Mikki parked behind Sophia's car. She could see Dante and Sophia standing on opposite sides of the kitchen and, judging by their body language, they were in the midst of a heated argument. She sat in the car, embarrassed to be watching but not ready to drive away and come back later. She'd had a long day. Finally she got out, slammed the driver's door, opened the trunk to retrieve her suitcase, and slammed that too. Dante stopped and said something to Sophia, who turned to look outside.

The argument wasn't new. Their disagreements usually began when Sophia was feeling as though she had to do everything at home *and* be a violinist, while Dante built furniture, showed up for meals, and—when convenient—helped with Holly. The key word was *convenient*.

Tonight's row was about yesterday morning. He had promised to take Holly to the 8 a.m. bus for summer camp because the orchestra wouldn't finish their Sunday performance until almost eleven and Sophia wouldn't get home until well after midnight. But when a new customer showed up just before eight o'clock, Dante took him to the office, and a tearful Holly rousted her mother out of bed. "I'm going to miss the bus, and I won't get to go to camp."

So much for sleeping in. Still wearing her pajamas, her hair in disarray, Sophia dropped her daughter off fifteen minutes late. Fortunately Holly wasn't the only camper who arrived late. The bus was still idling at the curb. Sophia silently fumed all Monday and Tuesday, finally boiling over just before Mikki returned. Part of the problem was that Sophia was bone tired. Summer was the busiest performance season; the other part was that Dante didn't notice she was fuming or realize he'd screwed up. Though he regularly promised to put Holly's needs into his work schedule, that promise had once again vaporized. She should have remembered to set her alarm clock.

Mikki walked to the back door slowly. By the time she was in the kitchen, Dante was gone.

Sophia gave her a quick hug, then rolled the suitcase to the guest room.

"Are you hungry? I can fix an omelet."

Mikki shook her head. "I bought a sandwich at the Food Court. I'm good. I do, however, need a shower and a decent night's sleep. I have therapy in the morning." She didn't want to talk about her weekend or her hand, and she was pretty sure Sophia didn't want to pretend to be interested. Any more than Mikki wanted to pretend she hadn't seen the argument.

Taylor Duncan's businesslike email showed up in Hank's inbox Tuesday evening. Just in time to interfere with his sleep.

FYI. I'm transferring back to Denver to take over the Denver office. Effective August 1st. Please give the girls a heads up. I'll be in touch. Taylor

Short and to the point. So like Taylor. This news explained why she hadn't yet made summer plans with the girls. Cate would probably be excited about having more access to the city. She was quick to complain about living in the sticks where nothing fun ever happened. He had to admit that having Taylor in Cate's life right now might help reduce some of the teenage snarky-ness he had no idea how to handle. His mother was trying to run interference, but even Grace's patience was wearing thin. Initially, Cate had welcomed the chance to work in the greenhouses. Her first paying job. But the shine was wearing off. Always on the lookout for ways to earn money, Erin offered to take her place and her paycheck. Cate was not amused.

Because Cate had just gotten her learner's permit, Hank let her drive out to his mother's. It was only five miles. Grace came out to the car, hugged the girls, and sent Cate off to the small greenhouse. "Manny's packing up today's orders." Erin grabbed her backpack and headed for the front porch. She had a new library book.

Grace gave her son a close look, "Not enough sleep?"

"Taylor's coming back to Denver."

"Permanently?"

"Who knows? She'll be heading up this branch."

"Do the girls know?"

He shook his head. "I need to get my head around it before I have to answer questions."

"Well, maybe more of Taylor might be what Cate needs now. Take some of the *all adults suck* attitude out of her. She was really on her high horse at Erin's party."

He remembered. "I've got to go. I'll pick them up a little after three. A patient cancelled. If your nerves can stand it, let Cate drive when you make your deliveries. Might improve her mood."

Grace frowned. "We'll see. Maybe on the way back."

One good thing about his job was that he couldn't ruminate about his own problems while he was working with patients. Today was the final appointment with Steve the skier. Hank was pleased with the results. Fortunately, the ski slopes wouldn't be open for a few more months, so Steve wouldn't be tempted to put too much strain on his knee for a while.

Mikki Richards arrived promptly at ten, looking as tired as Hank felt. If he remembered correctly, she flew back from Chicago yesterday.

As she settled herself in the chair and removed the brace, he asked, "How was your trip?"

"Okay." Nervously, she watched a frown take over his expression as he lightly touched the swollen area over her knuckles. Then turned her hand palm side up, assessing the damage.

Finally, "You played." Not a question.

She nodded.

"How long?"

"Maybe twenty minutes." *Closer to thirty, actually.*

"And?"

"A sharp pain." She pointed.

"Does it hurt now?"

"A little. I didn't take a pill this morning."

"But you did when it happened?"

"Yes."

"I need new X-rays. Let's see what you've done or undone." He was clearly annoyed.

Half an hour later, she returned to Hank's empty office to wait for the verdict, her stomach in a knot. Just before the end of her appointment hour, he walked in, fastened three X-rays to the light board, flipped the switch, and studied the images.

"See that," he pointed at her knuckles. "You've torn tendons, that's why it's swelling. So until it's healed, you can't continue with the exercises. Everything needs to rest. You've ruined a month's worth of work." He handed her the brace. "Wear it 24/7. And don't do anything with that hand."

"Driving?"

"Very little. I'll see you next Wednesday."

Dismissed.

She stood, "Thanks for not yelling."

"You're lucky. Someone else is at the top of my yelling list today."

If only it were possible to yell in an email.

With nothing to do—nothing she was allowed to do—Mikki was fairly sure she was going to go stark-staring mad. Holly was off enjoying camp, Sophia and Dante were either avoiding each other or being uncomfortably polite. Short term, Mikki was stuck. She needed the physical therapy, so leaving Evergreen wasn't an option. When Holly came home, there would be times when Sophia would need Mikki's help, especially on performance days.

But, assuming her hand got better and Holly was cared for, who would take a chance on a pianist whose hand might never be 100%? And at some point, Mikki needed a new path—one that provided income. Her checking account was currently healthy because she hadn't been spending her salary while she was in Europe. *Gaining Ground* had picked up the tab for almost everything. There might be a small profit from the condo, but she couldn't coast along on what she had. She wasn't accustomed to worrying about money.

Taylor Duncan wasn't surprised that Hank didn't respond to her email. Nothing in it required his input. She was certain he wasn't thrilled that she was coming back. She had chosen her career over her family, an opportunity to show what she could do in the New York financial world. No way to put a positive spin on what she'd done. Not only did she abandon her daughters—in truth, Hank was a better parent than she was—but she'd wrecked his chance at a surgical residency. Though she loved her girls, being a full-time mom couldn't compete with the accolades that came with bringing business to the brokerage, the challenge of making the right moves at the right time. And then there were the yearly bonuses.

Returning to Denver had never been in her playbook. Her first year in New York, she'd bought an impossibly expensive two-bedroom condo and learned the complexities of the subway system and the art of hailing taxis. She and her investment team annually out-performed most of the other teams. Then last year, Colin Talbot, the twice-divorced Broadway actor she'd been dating, proposed. The always pragmatic, rational Taylor Duncan was swept off her feet, immersed in the rarefied atmosphere of the theater. She introduced him to the girls via skype; she met his grown son over dinner at a popular sushi restaurant. All was well until, with no warning or explanation, he called the engagement off. Her fairy tale was over. There was nothing she could do or fix or call someone to fix. For a person who believed she was in control of her life, being dumped was a shock. Even worse, it was a very public dumping.

When the Denver slot opened up, she electioneered for the job. She needed to NOT be in New York where everyone in the theater and financial worlds were gossiping about the financial whiz and the Broadway icon. Social media feasted on the story. She was hurt and embarrassed. Angry at herself for being romantically gullible.

Going from the upper echelon in the New York office to managing the Denver office was a lateral move, but she'd really have preferred a managerial position in any city but Denver. The fallout from this move would be messy. There were still people in the Denver office who remembered her, people she'd climbed over to get her promotions. Now she would be their boss. Awkward didn't cover it.

In the meantime, there were other issues.

Renting her New York condo.

Renting something in Denver.

Changing the girls' visitation agreement. Though Hank hadn't answered her email, she knew he'd told Cate and Erin when Cate texted her:

So glad you're coming back.

Taylor hoped Cate understood coming back didn't mean staying in Denver permanently.

Hank had waited until Friday to tell his daughters that their mother was moving back to Denver. On his way home from the clinic, he picked up Chinese food. He needed the support of very spicy Kung Pau chicken to deliver the news. He knew Cate would be pleased. Erin less so. Having only been two when Taylor bailed, Erin didn't have the same kind of mom-memory Cate did. Somewhere along the line, Cate had put Taylor on a pedestal. Erin, however, was more interested in how Taylor's return would affect her own life.

Cate was excited, "I knew it."

Erin, ever the skeptic, "How did you know?"

"Social media has been all over the news that her Broadway lover boy broke off the engagement. Mom's love life has gone viral."

Hank had not known about that.

Erin was using chopsticks to eat her rice, with only occasional success. "I don't like all that twitting stuff. People say awful things."

"Your mother said she'll start her new job on August 1st, so she'll probably be in Denver a few days early. She'll let us know."

"Where will she live?" Erin gave up on the chopsticks and picked up her fork.

"No idea."

Cate, around her third spring roll, "I hope it's near downtown. There's more to do."

Erin frowned, "There's plenty to do here."

"No multiplexes, malls, or skating rinks."

"Who cares! What I want to know is where we are going to live. I don't want to change schools." Tears were threatening. Erin was good at looking for worse case scenarios.

"I might like a different high school."

"You just want more boys to choose from."

Hank felt the beginning of a headache, one that was going to stick around.

Within one week, Mikki had two offers on her condo. She took the higher one and went into escrow. She would have a profit, maybe between $30,000 and $35,000. Not enough to live on for long. While she was grateful the sale would go through, it also slammed a door. Humpty Dumpty could not be put together again. All the traveling with *Gaining Ground* had been exciting. Now she'd been cut loose from that kind of belonging. Adrift.

She knew her father would not be pleased about the sale—and he wasn't—but she needed a cash cushion. Investing it for the future was a luxury she couldn't afford. She had car and storage unit payments, as well as payments to Sophia for room and board. She probably needed a menial job to tide her over until her hand was healed—hopefully by fall, winter at the latest.

Evergreen's economy was mostly tourist related, though it was becoming an upscale bedroom for Denver. She doubted that Sophia or Hank would know much about local jobs. Dante might but she was giving him and Sophia space to sort out what was wrong between them. They didn't need any more of her troubles than they were already putting up with. She needed neutral counsel, so she went looking for Grace Duncan.

Mikki found her in the office inside the small greenhouse, staring at a computer screen. Mikki knocked lightly on the doorframe, "Grace?" Pulling off her reading glasses, Grace turned and smiled. "Are you too busy? I can come back some other time."

"Not at all—grab a chair." She motioned to several straight-backed chairs. "They're not all that comfortable. This office just sort of grew—like Topsy. I keep meaning to fix it up, but I'd rather take care of my plants than decorate or do paperwork."

"No problem, I've spent most of my life on uncomfortable piano benches. At least this has a back," she hesitated. Now that she was here, she was second-guessing herself. Grace slid the laptop to one side.

"How can I help you?"

In her generation, Grace Duncan had undoubtedly been too tall, maybe even labeled plain. Now in her early sixties, her height was in style, no gray evident in her auburn hair. She was wearing Levi's that had been washed once too often and a sleeveless plaid blouse that had a smudge of soil at the neck. Her eyes—which Hank had inherited—were her best feature, giving Mikki her full attention.

"I'm guessing most of the town knows the story of my hand. It's probably going to be a while before I can earn my living as a musician and since you know this area—I, well I need a temporary job that I can do with one good hand and one," she lifted her left arm slightly, "one that isn't too useful. During college I worked as a bartender in the summers, but that's a two-handed job. Your son won't speculate on how long the healing will take. I'm hoping it might be the first of next year. Anyhow, he's barely speaking to me because I tried playing while I was gone. I'm on his disobedient list."

Grace laughed. "I can imagine. Hank takes his work seriously. However his current grumpiness might not be because of you. He's dealing with his ex relocating to Denver."

Mikki waited.

"Let me ask around. Do you have to keep the brace on?"

"Yes. 24/7, only removed for showers. And let me tell you this thing itches."

Grace pushed a notepad toward Mikki. "Leave me your cell number. Is Mikki your given name?"

Mikki shook her head. "It's actually Marguerite. When I was learning to talk, I couldn't get all the sounds right. The closest I could get was Mikki. And it stuck. Probably more appropriate for a jazz pianist. Marguerite is too refined."

Grace laughed. "I'll call if I find something."

Mikki knew Noah didn't intend for his email to be upsetting, but it was. He was fitting himself into a new musical group. And she wasn't, couldn't. Might never again have the chance.

It's an okay bunch, just not like it was with Jay. Having been part of *Gaining Ground* has however given me a bit of status. They envy me for having played in so many places, being part of a Grammy-winning album. We practice Wednesday, Thursday, and Friday afternoons, perform Friday, Saturday and Sunday nights. It's weird to be in the same place for every performance. I finally found a decent apartment. A mile or so west of the French Quarter. Probably going to need some transportation, maybe a motorcycle. What do you think?

How's your hand? Can you visit or stay? I miss you. I have an extra bedroom.

That was probably the longest message Noah had ever written to her. At least he seemed happy, moving ahead. No mention of a girl, but there would be one soon. Noah was not given to celibacy.

Glad you're settling in. I'm still stuck. My impromptu performance in Chicago set the therapy back. In another week, it'll start again.

My sister's marriage is going through a bad patch. I wish I had somewhere else to stay, but I'm sort of needed to take care of my niece when Sophia's working.

I miss you too. Visiting isn't an option until the therapy is over.

My condo is in escrow and, don't laugh, I'm looking for a temporary job that doesn't require using my left hand all that much.

Holly came home from camp bubbling over with the wonders of learning to kayak and going on an overnight campout. She was quick to remind everyone that day-to-day life in Evergreen was, by comparison, boring. Mikki empathized. She was bored too. And stressed.

Though she wasn't supposed to do much driving, she drove Holly to Greeley to stay with Jon and Ardith. Mikki stayed one night, Holly stayed three. Tuesday, Sophia picked Holly up after rehearsal and they did some early back-to-school shopping in Denver. Mikki was beginning to see the wisdom of year-round schools. Not something she'd ever cared about. An entire summer of unstructured time for children with two working parents wasn't practical. Turning kids loose had gone out of fashion when helicopter parenting arrived.

Mikki's first return-to-therapy appointment coincided with Grace Duncan's text: **I might have a lead.**

I can come after I leave the clinic. 11:30?

Yes.

Today, Hank seemed less annoyed with the condition of her hand. He even smiled once or twice. There were more X-rays. He mapped out a time line and gave her a new series of exercises. She wondered about his problems with his ex but was sure he wouldn't appreciate his mother having told her about his private life.

As soon as Hank sent her on her way, she drove to Grace's, parking near the greenhouses. Grace was sitting in her office, talking to a stocky, balding man in bib overalls.

Grace smiled when she saw Mikki. "Glad you could come. This is my assistant, Manny Aguilar. Manny, meet Mikki Richards, one of Hank's patients."

Manny reached to shake her hand. "Hi, " taking note of the brace, "so the left arm is what Hank's working on?"

"My hand."

"What happened?"

"An argument with a bus seat." Providing details about the crash still made her uncomfortable.

"Ouch."

Mikki nodded.

Manny turned back to Grace, "I have to finish moving the bulbs. Let me know when you want to leave, and I'll load the van."

Grace smiled at Mikki, "Would you like coffee?"

"I had some at the clinic."

Grace made a face. "That can NOT be called coffee. I keep telling Hank he's trying to kill his patients."

Mikki laughed. "It is terrible. After spending a year in Europe, I've been spoiled by really good coffee."

"Mine's slightly better than the clinic's. I bought a Keurig. No guessing."

"Some other time."

"Have a seat and let me tell you about the job. It's perhaps more temporary than you want. Ella, the sister of one of my florist customers, is pregnant and due any day. She's a hostess at the Alpine Brewery in Idaho Springs and needs someone to fill in until she can get back. Maybe a month. It doesn't pay all that well because the tips go to the wait-staff. You need to seat people, provide menus, run the cash register and the credit card thingy. No heavy lifting. What do you think?"

"It's a place to start. Any idea about hours?"

Grace shook her head. "The manager is Gus Winslow. Ella gave him your name." She handed Mikki a business card. "His number is on the back."

Mikki was momentarily torn between gratitude for Grace's effort and embarrassment. From performing in Rome to hourly work in Idaho Springs. Humbling.

When things changed, they really changed.

Before calling for an interview, she needed to know Sophia's schedule. She found her sister in the laundry room, folding towels. "Hostessing? Why would you want a job like that?"

"I need something that doesn't require doing much with my left hand."

Sophia added the last towel to the laundry basket. "Are you short of money?"

"Not exactly short, but nothing is coming in."

Mikki knew Sophia and everyone else thought she'd been getting rich with the band. Not really the case, except maybe for Jay. The band made big bucks but also wracked up huge expenses. Traveling first class whenever possible. However, when they weren't working, they weren't getting paid.

"What about the money from the condo?"

"Some help. But it won't last all that long."

Over lunch—another one of Sophia's salads—they laid out the weeks remaining until Holly was back in school and twice-weekly soccer practice resumed. The after school study hall in the cafeteria was also available if neither Sophia nor Dante could pick her up. So there would be fewer days for Mikki to cover.

"I first have to get the job, but at least I can make an educated guess about whether the hours will work for Holly."

Mikki really wished Sophia would stop with all the salads. A grilled cheese sandwich would have been gratefully received.

Her appointment with Gus Winslow was just before the Brewery's 11 a.m. opening on Friday. With a name like Gus, Mikki had imagined someone older, not a clean-shaven thirty-something with a blond ponytail and wire-rimmed glasses, reminiscent of John Denver. He was working behind a long, highly polished bar that displayed all the micro-beer choices.

The dining room and bar were separated by a wide entry area. The bar had two long tables with a series of short benches, Colorado's imitation of a German-style beer garden. The dining area was a mixture of booths and tables. Wagon wheels and rusty farm tools on the walls, along with enlarged, sepia-toned historical photos of Idaho Springs. Blue gingham tablecloths.

Gus led her to a table by a picture window that overlooked the street. "Would you like something to drink?"

"Maybe ice water?" Despite being in the mountains, midday temperatures were in the 80's.

Gus signaled the girl who was setting up the tables.

"Ella said you're recovering from an accident," he gestured toward the brace.

"Physical therapy for my hand. I can take the brace off but can't do anything strenuous with my hand. It's going to take several more weeks of therapy. I'm staying in Evergreen with my sister's family."

The young waitress brought a tall glass of ice water. Gus pushed his chair back a little. "The dining room is where you'll work. Bar patrons pay at the bar, then seat themselves. He slid a laminated menu across the table. As soon as the dining room customers are seated and have their menus, you can go back to the reception area. When they're finished, they pay you at the front counter. That's it. We don't take checks or reservations. The line can get quite long in the evening, so you have to keep impatient customers happy. The restaurant's land line is in my office so you won't have to answer it." He studied her for a moment, "Does that sound workable?"

"It does. What about the hours? I often need to take care of my niece."

"Ella works Monday and Tuesday nights and Wednesday, Thursday and Friday lunches, 11-3. Her counterpart, Susie, does the rest. Perhaps you could come in tomorrow and shadow Susie during the lunch shift. Then we can see where we are." He made it all sound easy, though there would undoubtedly be hiccups. He walked her to the door. "Bring your Social Security info and another ID so we can do the paperwork."

Simpler than she imagined.

That afternoon, a brown envelope with the *Gaining Ground* return address arrived in the mail. Mikki assumed it was more legal documents about the band. Instead, it was a folder with two of her rough compositions with notes around the edges in Jay's familiar, cramped handwriting. She teared-up.

A 3" x 5" yellow post-it was on the top sheet. **Mikki: I found these in the stacks of music Jay had in his briefcase. I thought you'd want to see his notes. More may turn up. I'm still sorting. Neatness was not his long suit. Love, Teri**

Mikki had been experimenting with composing since high school, taking as many musi-comp classes as she had time for at the university. During their last tour, Jay had been mentoring her and had written lyrics for these two pieces. Melodies had always followed her around, but adding words was not her thing. She pushed the pillows against the bed's headboard and sank into them, still holding the precious pages, remembering the best time in her life. Seven years of becoming a professional musician, being part of a creative group. Learning to perform in front of huge crowds and work in a recording studio. Hanging out with the guys.

Tears seeped, then flowed. She set the pages aside so they wouldn't get wet and let sorrow consume her. When they'd told her Jay was dead, she'd been coming out of the anesthesia. He'd been her friend and mentor. Since then, she'd seldom cried, burying her grief about him and her hand, afraid to think ahead. It hurt to remember the past. Now she was holding an envelope containing what was left of her musical life.

Sunday afternoon, Mikki worked up the courage to go into Sophia's studio, close the door, and sit at the piano that had once been her mother's. The piano she had learned on. She was wearing her brace so she wouldn't be tempted to use her left hand. Hank's warnings were still loud and clear. She arranged two of the sheets Teri had sent on the rack, studying her original notations and the comments Jay had added. Slowly, she picked out the melody, resurrecting what she'd heard all those months ago. Then stopped, looked at Jay's notes, and began incorporating his suggestions one measure at a time. There were chord suggestions for the bass clef too, but they'd have to wait until she could use her left hand. She knew he would not push her to revise something unless she liked what he offered. Jay believed that everyone heard music differently and should follow their instincts.

In these minutes, it was as though he were here, in her head. Unexpectedly comforting.

She left the studio after half an hour. The family was due back from visiting friends, and Mikki didn't want to call attention to what she was doing—partially because she wasn't sure what she was doing. Playing her music, touching it with the keys, was a way of reminding herself that even if she had only one functioning hand, she was still a musician.

She was sitting on the porch swing when the Perillos returned. It was rare that the three of them went someplace together. Maybe an effort to smooth over what was definitely a bumpy summer.

Holly raced onto the porch. "Look what I have! Two tickets to Jazz at the Lake House for next Sunday. For you and me from one of Dad's customers. I'd love to go and you know about jazz—do you want to go?"

Dante had already disappeared into his workshop while Sophia followed her daughter to the porch. "She's been asking to go to the festival for a couple of years."

Mikki looked at the tickets and the colorful flyer Holly handed her.

"Do you know who these people are? Mom says you might not. The tickets are for a band called *Yesterday's Blues*."

As always, Holly's energy was catching. "I'd love to." Listening to jazz might be just what Mikki needed to distract herself. Her first shift at

the brewery was the Monday after the performance, and she was oddly
nervous.

Holly was ready an hour before the performance, wearing one of
her new "for school" outfits, denim leggings, a peasant style blouse, and
sandals.

"Can we go early and watch everything set up?"

"Yes, but they might not let us in until they are set up."

Before Holly exploded with anticipation, Mikki gave in and they were
at the Lake House door twenty minutes early.

The concert was sold out. The venue seated 150, small when compared
to most of *Gaining Ground's* concerts in the last few years.

Mikki had only seen the Lake House from a distance. It was built
entirely of old growth logs burnished into a warm raw sienna. The
mountains of the Front Range and Evergreen Lake forming a backdrop.
Inside, the walls and vaulted ceiling were exposed logs. At one end,
floor to roof windows brought the mountains inside. A massive natural
stone fireplace dominated one wall. Otherwise, there were no permanent
fixtures since the House was used for all sorts of entertainment: weddings,
quinceaneras, graduations, and of course intimate musical performances.
Today, there were rows of white folding chairs arranged across the
middle, seat numbers taped to the backs. The band had set themselves
up in front of the windows, only instruments and microphones as staging.

Their seats were at the end of the ninth row. Mikki put Holly on the
aisle so, if she didn't sit still, no one else would be disturbed, though jazz
audiences were not always quiet anyway. People spontaneously jumping
up to dance in the aisles.

Holly couldn't look at everything fast enough. "Do you recognize
any of them?"

Mikki shook her head.

"Will anyone recognize you?"

Again Mikki shook her head.

"Maybe it's because your hair is different."

"Normally, people only recognized Jay."

"Why do they have so many cords all over the floor?"

"They're for the microphones and amplifiers. And the electric guitar."

"How come it's only guys? No girls."

A white-haired woman two rows ahead turned around to give Holly a stern look.

Mikki mouthed *Sorry* to the woman.

"Hol, keep your voice down."

The performance lasted nearly two hours with no intermission. The group played a little of everything: predominately blues, some swing, New Orleans jazz as well as contemporary jazz. Mikki yearned to be up there.

As she and Holly left the building, the tall, blond bass player caught up with them. "Excuse me. Are you Mikki Richards?"

Mikki turned, surprised someone recognized her.

"Yes."

"I thought so. Noah Stein showed me your picture and said I should be on the lookout for you. That you two go way back and you just might come to the jazz festival since you're local now."

"How do you know him?"

"Our band spends half the year in New Orleans. It's a tight music scene. You should come."

"And you are?"

Holly eagerly held up the program, which she'd already turned to his picture. "You're Lyle Anders. Can I have your autograph?"

"Of course." He pulled a pen from his shirt pocket. "Your name is?"

"Holly Perillo." She spelled both names. "Mikki is my aunt."

He scrawled his signature across his picture. "Thank you for asking. Bass players don't always get a lot of attention." He handed the program back to Holly.

"How's Noah doing?"

"Getting acclimated. He's a great talent."

"Yes."

"Well, I've gotta get my stuff back to the van. We're heading into Canada for two weeks. I'll tell Noah I found you." And he was gone.

"Wow," Holly was impressed. "He knew you." She carefully refolded the program.

"A friend of mine put him up to it. Not quite the same as fan appreciation. Let's grab hamburgers at Cactus Jack's."

"Yea! I want the *Airplane* hamburger."

The restaurant was jammed with day-trippers from Denver and summer tourists, so it took a while to get waited on. As they exited the restaurant, they saw Hank walking across the parking lot. Mikki always expected him to be in his white coat, but today he was in faded Levi's and a black t-shirt. A macho look that surprised her.

As usual, Holly was full of questions: "Where's Erin?"

"In Denver with her sister and mother."

"I thought their mother lived in New York."

Mikki tried one of Sophia's parenting tricks. She handed Holly the car keys. "Why don't you wait for me in the car. I'll just be a minute."

As she walked away, Holly's body language suggested a huge sulk might be coming.

"Sorry. She's been wound up all afternoon. A woman in the audience even gave her the evil eye for talking too much, and she got one of the band members to give her an autograph."

"I understand. Both of mine were wired because they're visiting their mother for a week."

"So you're temporarily child-free."

"Yeah. It'll be great for one day, and then the house will seem weirdly silent. Did you enjoy the concert?"

"How can anyone not enjoy jazz? I was converted at the age of eight."

"Did you join them on stage against my orders about playing?"

She was instantly defensive, "No." Then realized he was teasing. "I was tempted, but it's not a good idea to join a performance unless you're invited."

"And you weren't."

"I was not."

"Good. Well, I need to pick up my order. At least I won't have to share my fries. See you on Wednesday."

By the time Hank got home, his food had cooled off. French fries were so much better hot. Warming them up just dried them out. A fitting end to an uncomfortable afternoon. Being face to face with Taylor was always stressful. Not that they argued publicly, but they were awkwardly careful—tiptoeing around past injuries so as not to upset the girls. Seven plus years and Hank hadn't gotten over his anger at what she'd done to their family and his career. Having her back in Denver was the absolute last thing he needed. Truth be told, it was probably not where Taylor wanted to end up either.

Hank would have preferred to drop the girls off at Taylor's door and beat a hasty retreat.

Instead, the girls hugged their mother and hurried away to check out their new bedrooms, leaving their parents to stumble through the moment. He took note of the storage containers in the living room. "Unpacking is a slow process."

"I did the girls' rooms first."

"Did you buy or are you renting?"

"Renting. I'm also renting my New York apartment. Not ready to burn bridges yet."

No surprise. Hank was pretty sure she was simply waiting until the furor in New York abated. Unfortunately, the girls had no way of knowing this was just an interlude. Taylor never noticed that she was stepping on other people's lives. He hadn't picked up on her *me first* attitude until Erin's birth. The girls would once again come in second.

He and Taylor met at a Greek Rush Week party during their Freshman year at Boulder. Hank wasn't interested in pledging a fraternity but his roommate was, so Hank tagged along for the free food and beer. His Pre-Med studies and part-time job in the campus bookstore would take up all of his time.

Taylor was hands-down the prettiest girl in the room. A natural blonde, her hair reaching below her shoulders, parted in the middle. Tall, maybe 5' 7" or 8". Unlike some tall men, Hank wasn't drawn to short girls. To complement her looks, she had a sharp wit and a smile that he thought about for days. Soon he was spending all his free time with her.

Now, twenty years later, he was checking his watch, wanting to put space between them. "Text me what time I should pick them up next weekend."

"Probably Saturday afternoon. I have to get ready to be at work early Monday. Anything going on with them that I should know about?"

"Cate has hated working in the greenhouses, and both of them are expecting a shopping day for school clothes."

"Already on the agenda."

Nothing more to be said.

"Hey guys," he raised his voice, "I'm leaving."

Cate yelled, "Bye!" Erin, however, raced out of her room to give him a hug. "Love you."

As he opened the door, Taylor thanked him for delivering the girls, and the awkward family reunion was over. He'd read about divorced couples who eventually became friends, smoothing the edges for the children. But he and Taylor had never come close to post-marital friendship. Hank wondered whether they had ever been friends, lovers certainly, no problem with that aspect of their relationship. Since the split, they'd never managed anything except polite tolerance.

In hindsight, the timing of their marriage had been wrong, interfering with both career paths. Taylor wanted to wheel and deal, to conquer the financial world. He wanted to help patients heal. Had always wanted that. He also loved being a father. The demands of his residency wouldn't work with the responsibility of being a single father. His two-year old and seven-year-old daughters needed him, so the medical world was going to have to do without him. Leaving the residency was the hardest thing he'd ever done. Harder than signing the divorce papers.

Taylor probably had never enjoyed motherhood. Her first pregnancy wasn't planned, but they'd coped. Her salary and bonuses covered their living expenses; Hank's scholarship filled in everything else. By the time Cate was in kindergarten, the marital cracks had already begun. Who was going to go to parent/teacher conferences? Who would drop her off at school and pick her up? More often than not, it was Hank.

Several months in marriage counseling trying to resurrect their initial attraction only resulted in Taylor getting pregnant with Erin. Another child to get in the way of Taylor's rise to the top. Erin was almost three when Taylor handed him the divorce papers. "I'm not cut out for this."

No apology, then or since. She was quite willing to let him make the day-to-day decisions. Not the life he'd imagined. But the girls deserved at least one parent and a very kind grandmother.

Mikki's first two nights at Alpine Brewing were exhausting but, for the most part, uneventful. Because people visiting a restaurant are generally good-humored, the buoyant cacophony in both the bar and restaurant didn't allow time for anything except smiling and asking, "How many are in your party?" then figuring out which table would be suitable.

The hardest part was driving back to Sophia's at night. The road was pitch dark, and Mikki kept having to raise and lower the headlight beams. She prayed there wouldn't be any deer to contend with.

When she walked into therapy on Wednesday, an hour earlier than usual, a small keyboard was set up alongside the examination table. She didn't want to appear too eager, so she went with "Do you want a lesson?"

He grinned. "Sure, but first you have to pass an exam."

Always a catch.

He rolled his chair across to the table and removed her brace, studying her hand, gently massaging her palm and fingers.

"Any pain?"

"No."

"Good." He pulled the keyboard around so she was facing it.

She touched middle C with her right index finger. "Sounds good, though keyboards don't have the rich sound a piano does."

"Getting someone to loan me a piano wasn't an option. I borrowed this from one of Cate's friends."

"I wasn't complaining."

"Start slowly and gently play a scale or two. I want to watch how you use your hand."

Mikki lightly placed her hands on the keys and played a quick scale with her right hand.

Hank watched with interest. "So the thumb goes beneath the first three fingers."

"An octave has seven keys; I have only five fingers."

Almost a smile, "Now that we've established I don't know anything about the piano, do the same thing with your left hand. Slowly." Again, he studied the move and had her repeat it five times. "How does your hand feel? And do not say *fine*."

She thought about his question. "Maybe tight."

"Umm." He pulled the keyboard over so he was facing it and played a scale with his left hand.

Mikki was impressed that he wanted to replicate what she did with her hand so he could help her. His hand was certainly stronger, broader across the knuckles. He could easily reach an octave.

"Does it hurt when you cross over?"

"No. Like I said, just tight. I can easily reach an octave, C to C, with my right hand." She demonstrated. "But not with my left." She could only span seven keys.

"Can all pianists make that reach with both hands?"

"Probably not, but I always could."

He sat, studying her hand on the keyboard. "Do you have a video of you playing, when you're making fast, complex moves?"

"No, but maybe Teri does. I'll call the band's office."

"I'd like to see how your hand moves when you're performing so I can determine what kinds of strain playing puts on the muscles and tendons."

Not only was Teri happy to hear from Mikki but, coincidentally, she had just received DVDs of their Rome performance. "One copy for everyone in the band, one for me, and the master in case I need to make more. I'll put yours in the mail tomorrow."

Teri went on to tell Mikki all the news about the band members, the support crew, and the fact that her drummer had proposed. She hadn't given him an answer yet. By the time Teri explained all the career changes for the band, Mikki wanted to crawl into bed and pull the comforter over her head. The guys had new jobs, maybe not as good as being with Jay but they were performing. Noah in New Orleans, Earle in Chicago, Buddy in LA.

Without previewing the DVD, Mikki brought it to her next appointment.

Hank slipped it into the player. It opened to a drone's eye view of the Parco. Hank leaned in to get a closer look. "That's a huge theater. How many does it seat?"

"Three thousand or so."

And suddenly, there was Jay, center stage, with his guitar, the camera panning across Noah, Earle, Buddy.

And Mikki at the piano.

Her life. Her friends. Their music. In Hank's office. The sounds washing over her, at once familiar and excruciating. The loss that had been muted all these months pushed to the surface, her silent tears spilling and spilling.

"I can't." She stood up. "I'll wait outside."

But before she got out the door, Hank had switched it off and was holding her against him, her tears spotting his white coat. That life was gone forever, no way to put it back together, no way to put herself back together. She let him hold her, her arms at her sides, like a rag doll.

When she was quieter, he guided her back to her chair, squatting in front of her, holding her hands. Eventually the sobs became hiccups, diminishing a little at a time. Hank didn't know what to say. Had no clear idea how to help this kind of pain. Tears in children were easier to cope with; tears in women were always intimidating. In the weeks she'd been coming for therapy, he'd only seen her determination to recover. At this moment, he was witnessing vulnerability, the depth of her distress at being deprived of the world she'd been part of.

He knew what that loss felt like. When Taylor walked away from their marriage, his surgical career came to a screeching halt. A change over which he had no control. Mikki had no control over the bus that crashed. She was where he had been seven years ago.

The crying left her dazed. From a distance she heard Hank ask, "Should I call the restaurant and tell them you won't be in this morning?"

She shook her head.

"You're in no shape to drive or work."

"I need to go." Anything to take her mind off her memories.

He studied her, her face wet, eyes puffy and red. "Are you sure?"

She nodded.

He stood up, helped her stand. "Why don't you wash your face?"

Hank recruited Betty to drive her to Idaho Springs. As Mikki got out of the car, "I'll pick you up after your shift. Boss's orders."

When Betty pulled into the clinic's parking lot mid-afternoon, Mikki thanked her, got into her own car, and drove to Sophia's, grateful no one was at the house or in Dante's workshop. She took a long shower and stretched out on her bed, emotionally exhausted. Seeing Jay so full of joy, playing and singing, she longed to be back on a stage—any stage—to feel the rush of sound. She missed riding the high of creating something beautiful.

Since elementary school, music had been her obsession. The usual things most women were supposed to want—a man, a child—would have to come later, if at all. She'd seldom had close women friends. The band members were her friends. Without music and them, she was alone. Alone.

She didn't know what to do with that truth.

When she woke, it was dark outside. At a distance, she could hear the voices on the TV and Holly laughing. Maybe Sophia had been wiser. She had music *and* a life. For the first time ever, Mikki envied her sister.

Mikki was scheduled to see Dr. Conroy in another week for an evaluation of the therapy. She'd been secretly and carefully playing on Sophia's piano. Choosing pieces with easy bass parts, what she dubbed half-playing. If it turned out that there was no more that could be done, her reason for staying in Evergreen was over. Her job at Alpine was also ending. Ella had given birth to a boy and would soon be returning to work, fortunate to have a sister to look after the baby. Mikki was toying with the possibility of going to New Orleans, taking Noah up on his email invitation. She needed to talk to him, have him evaluate her playing, needed to be in a music environment again before her soul shriveled completely.

Because both Sophia and Dante had work commitments, Mikki accompanied Holly to the fifth grade orientation day. She'd overheard them arguing about who would take Holly to school. Mikki volunteered so that Holly could meet her new teacher, find her classroom, and pick up her textbooks. One of the waitresses at the restaurant was covering for her.

While Holly was in her classroom, Mikki waited on a schoolyard bench where Hank found her. Because he was carrying coffee while scrolling on his phone, he didn't see her until he was a few feet away and she spoke to him. "Good morning. No patients today?"

Startled, he stopped scrolling and looked up. "No, I kept the calendar clear. You brought Holly?"

"I'm the fall-back person when her parents are too busy and unable to compromise." A situation that refused to go away.

"My mother—my fall-back person—is booked to take Cate to the high school orientation on Monday. Her last words were *You owe me.*"

He sat beside her. "I don't remember orientations when I was in school. What about you?"

She shook her head. "We showed up on the first day and hit the ground, running."

"Did you like school? Erin mostly endures it so she can play soccer. A bribe to keep her working for C's. Right now the bar is set low."

"Holly's just the opposite. Sort of obsessive about getting A's."

He shifted a little so he could look at Mikki more directly; the intensity of his eyes holding onto hers was different from the way he looked at her during therapy sessions—good different. "You didn't answer my question."

"I liked parts. Music of course, Math, because you need math for music—and history."

"Why history?"

She shrugged. "I wanted to know what I missed all those years ago."

He smiled. "For instance?"

"The Oregon Trail. I know it was grueling, but everything was new for those people. I'd have liked the adventure," she paused, "I'm assuming you were a good student; I mean, you're in medicine."

"Yeah. A science nerd but I also liked being outdoors. Did lots of camping with my family. Did you ever camp?"

She shook her head. "My dad's an academic who thinks libraries are exciting, so that would be *no*. Holly loved her experiences camping out this summer."

"There's nothing better, well almost nothing."

"Do you take your daughters camping?"

"No. Their mother hates doing anything where you might get dirty. And since I've had the girls full time, I rarely take time off."

At that moment, they spotted Erin and Holly walking toward them, laughing.

Hank waved. "Shall we take them to Cactus Jack's?"

"Good idea." She was learning that, away from the clinic, he was good company. As well as good looking. Not once did he ask about her hand.

The girls begged to have a table all to themselves, so Hank and Mikki found a booth where they could keep an eye on them. Hank moved the mound of French fries he and Mikki had ordered to the center of the table, "Ranch or ketchup?"

Mikki made a face. "Ranch, never. Ketchup please."

"What's wrong with Ranch?"

"So many things. Where should I start?"

"You and Cate have something in common."

"Tell me about Cate."

He wiped his fingers on the napkin and took a few minutes to answer.

"Well—she's a teenager, so that means all adults are annoying about everything. I worry that spending more time with her mother might not be good. Taylor has never quite figured out how to set boundaries or listen. Cate's a good student, really good in math and science."

"A boyfriend?"

"No one special yet. I've been spared that. She wants a car for her sixteenth birthday. No way I can afford that, but I bet she'll guilt Taylor into it. And then I'll really have something to worry about."

At that moment, their hamburgers arrived.

That evening, replaying the events of the day, Hank found himself thinking about Mikki—not as a rather stubborn patient but as an interesting, sometimes funny woman who was good company and attractive. He did have to remind himself she was still a patient and he should maintain that separation. But his mind wasn't cooperating. Today, she had triggered a response that he hadn't anticipated, hadn't felt with anyone in quite a while. He wondered whether she'd noticed.

She had. So, when Dr. Conroy cancelled the therapy sessions, and Hank asked her if she'd accompany him on a Sunday afternoon drive to Georgetown—*We might get good fall color*—she accepted. She didn't want to shut down whatever might be brewing between them even though she'd be leaving soon. There was something quietly magnetic about him.

"Great. I'll pick you up about eleven."

"What about the girls?"

"Cate will be at home with Erin—I'm not allowed to say *babysitting*. Because Cate didn't have money to buy me a birthday present, she gave me ten *Sitting Coupons*. I redeemed one."

"How often do they go to Denver?"

"Every other weekend."

"Do you always do the chauffeuring?"

"Taylor doesn't have a car. She got used to taxis and Uber in New York. Besides, she doesn't like venturing into the back of beyond. She prefers all things city."

Mikki listened for bitterness or anger in his words but didn't find either one.

She was looking forward to Sunday. Hank's shift from therapist to good-looking single father was intriguing. There was a steadiness about him. Comfortable in his own skin.

The appointment with Dr. Conroy had loomed as a benchmark of sorts. More therapy? Another surgery?

Mikki's secret practicing already told her that the hand could do the basics without the brace. Only mild discomfort if she limited her playing time. She hoped that might indicate healing. Hank had given her the envelope with the most recent X-rays and reminded her to be honest about her hand. "Call my cell when you're done." She was touched by his concern.

During the appointment, Mikki's stomach was in a knot. She so wanted a clean bill of health, wanted to be told she was ready to get back to her musical work. But wanting rarely made something happen.

Dr. Conroy's voice was measured. "It's much better than it was three months ago."

Mikki knew that. Three months ago she couldn't hold a full coffee mug. Now she could. Three months ago, she couldn't play without tightness, sometimes pain. Now she could. Maybe not day-after-day.

"But—" Dr. Conroy laid the X-rays aside.

Mikki tensed.

"It's probably not going to be 100% for a long time. Keep up with whatever exercises you're doing. Most importantly, don't go back to playing like you did with the band."

"So this is as good as it'll be." Mikki fought to keep disappointment out of her voice.

"No telling. The bones and muscles are healed enough for daily activities, like getting dressed or washing your hair. Using your hand for jazz performances," Dr. Conroy paused, "don't count on it."

8

Mikki was waiting on Sophia's front porch when Hank arrived, driving the smaller of Duncan Gardens' delivery vans. Once she'd fastened her seatbelt, "We're delivering?"

"Picking up bulbs from one of my mother's suppliers in Georgetown. I'm repaying her for driving Cate to orientation. It'll only take a few minutes. Then we can have lunch and take a look around."

"Sounds good." It really did. She'd never been a fan of date dates. Reservations at high-end restaurants, getting dressed up, having to be on her best behavior. Too contrived. Today was more her style. Hank was wearing Levi's and an unbuttoned plaid flannel shirt over a t-shirt. She'd chosen denim leggings and a fleece top. The crisp breeze was a reminder that it was autumn in the high country and cooler days were at hand.

Hank was concentrating on the I-70 traffic, which was surprisingly heavy for a Sunday, and Mikki was enjoying the scenery, appreciating that they were both comfortable with silence. Immediately after they exited the Interstate, Hank turned south for a mile or so, pulling into the gravel drive in front of High Altitude Nursery, a hodge-podge of small greenhouses behind a bright orange prefab shed. "Stay here. Let me find someone."

Mikki watched him stride toward the garish shed, reemerging with a teenage boy in work boots and bib overalls. They disappeared into one of the greenhouses and, in a few minutes, the boy was pushing a cart of flats filled with small pots. Hank opened the sliding door behind Mikki's seat, placed the bulbs inside, then signed some paperwork.

Back in the truck, "Time to look for lunch." He turned the van around and headed into the town with its rows of false-front shops squeezed between the mountains, ending at a lake. The sign at the edge of the main street read **Entering Georgetown Historical District, Altitude 8,540 ft**.

Another sign below directed visitors to the Loop Train west of town. Mikki suddenly remembered: "My fifth grade class came here to ride the train. Isn't there a really high trestle somewhere?"

"Devil's Gate. A big deal in its day. I've never ridden the train. I was always bored with anything that seemed touristy. My dad however loved the old steam trains. His father worked in the round house in Durango when my dad was in grade school."

"Did you grow up in Evergreen?"

"Boulder. My dad was an accountant. When he passed on, my mom used the insurance money to build her greenhouses. She'd been working part time for a commercial nursery. She supplies flowers for *The Bloomin' Fool* and *Flowers Galore*. The bulbs we picked up are paper whites. They're popular during the holidays."

"I don't know much about flowers—except the bouquets we'd get after performances. Actually I don't know much about keeping house, cooking or gardening."

"Just music."

"Ummm. The poster child for putting all your eggs in one basket."

Hank let the opening pass. Today was not about her injury. He wanted to get to know her in a different way.

He parked on a side street and they walked back, reading menus posted in the restaurant windows, weighing the merits of the offerings. They finally chose a restaurant with a patio that had heat lamps to hold off the breeze.

Mikki ordered a BLT and beer.

"Beer?" He seemed genuinely surprised.

"Why not?"

"I would have guessed wine."

"When you're rehearsing hours and hours, beer is more practical. No fragile glass, just a bottle that can sit on the piano or the floor. Same for long bus rides. Bottles travel better."

He closed the menu and looked at the waitress. "Hamburger, medium, and a Tecate beer."

Mikki took note. "Is Tecate good?"

"Yes. Don't tell Coors. I'll be run out of the state."

She turned to the waitress. "I'll have Tecate too."

Hank liked that she was willing to experiment. Taylor thought drinking beer was common.

"Since we already know I'm musically ignorant, what was a rehearsal like? How often did you practice?"

Mikki crossed her arms along the edge of the table and gave herself a moment to walk—carefully—into the minefield that was her past.

"How often depended on our performances. If we were in between tours and working on new material, once a week, mayhe twice. If we were on tour, we'd probably warm up sometime during the day, an hour or so. Jay was always afraid of taking the edge off, being stale for the evening concert. Individually, most musicians practice a little everyday. I at least did scales and maybe ran one piece."

"No down time."

"Not entirely."

"How long were you together?"

"Over six years."

Once the orders came, they concentrated on the food and beer.

"Do you like it?" Hank pointed at her beer.

"It's different, but yes." This was the second lunch they'd shared, not counting the birthday cake at Grace's. During her PT sessions, he was intent, brusque at times. She liked the relaxed version better. There was a thoughtfulness, a measured-ness in his words.

She wondered what it would be like to kiss him.

They lingered over their lunch, ordered coffee, then drove to the lake, parking near a boat launch busy with Sunday fishermen.

Mikki asked, "Do you fish?"

He shook his head, "Not much for sitting in a boat all afternoon. Besides, if the water's rough, I get seasick. Lakesick. Truly humiliating. Then there's having to clean the fish."

Without a segue: "I'm going to New Orleans."

Hank let a minute or two pass. "When?"

"My last day at Alpine is on Friday and, since there are no more clinic appointments, probably next Sunday. I haven't made a reservation yet."

"Why there? I thought the band was headquartered in Chicago."

"There is no band. Everyone has scattered. Noah invited me. Now that he's found an apartment."

"The bass player?"

She nodded. "We've been friends since we were undergraduates."

"Just friends?" He meant to tease her but, too late, realized he might have overstepped.

"More than that for a while during our Junior year. Ultimately, we decided we preferred the friendship part."

He liked that the question didn't bother her.

"Are you going to look for work?"

"Yes. Noah's offered to help me make connections."

When Hank didn't say anything, she assumed he was worried about her hand. "I promise not to wreck all your hard work on my behalf."

"Good."

After another pause, "What?"

"I'll miss seeing you."

Taken aback, she chose lightness. "Do you say that to all your ex-patients?"

Instead of answering, "Do you need a ride to the airport? I have to pick the girls up in Denver Sunday afternoon."

"Yes I do, thanks. I don't have a flight yet."

"Let me know."

"Okay."

Later, she couldn't quite remember how the kiss began. Maybe when his hand touched her cheek, turning her to face him. Kissing in the front seat of a delivery van isn't especially easy, but the location didn't interfere with the quality of the kiss—gentle, then deep and more insistent. Warming them. Ending a little at a time.

He straightened in his seat and started the engine, reluctantly pushing the moment away. "Will you come back here?"

"I haven't thought that far." *Right now, not thinking at all.* Mikki fumbled with her seatbelt.

At least she knew that kissing him made her lightheaded.

Sophia had always been the sensible daughter, in spite of the fact that she preferred the violin to the piano. Her mother often joked that both her daughters had gone rogue when it came to following in their mother's steps. *I went wrong somewhere.*

Looking at her current life, Sophia was beginning to wonder where she and Dante had gone wrong. When they moved to Evergreen, she knew the commute to Denver would be difficult. Dante had promised her they'd make it work, but it wasn't working, primarily because, as his business had grown, he had less and less free time. His reputation as a master craftsman brought more and more orders until he couldn't manage on his own any longer. There were not only customers to think about but also two employees and endless paperwork. Family responsibilities slipped lower on Dante's list. From Sophia's perspective, it felt as though he didn't care about them. From his, he believed he was taking good care of his family. Perillo Woods was bringing in more than what Sophia was earning with the Symphony.

They went out of their way not to talk about the situation, about Holly's care or for that matter their relationship. Sex was perfunctory, if it happened at all. Some nights he didn't come to bed until well after midnight when Sophia was asleep. She was always the one to see that their daughter got to school. Sometimes, Holly rode the school bus home or one of the other mothers dropped her off. Too often, she was at home on her own. Mikki's arrival had temporarily pushed the problem of Holly's care to the back burner.

And now there was the possibility of Sophia being promoted to Principal of the second violins. The promotion would mean more money, more responsibility, and more time in Denver. She hadn't mentioned it to Dante. There seemed no right time, and Mikki would be leaving as soon as the therapy sessions ended. Thankfully, school was starting soon, but the underlying problems couldn't be solved by after school activities. Sophia and Dante were out of step. In trying to juggle everything, they were damaging what mattered.

By being persistent, Mikki finally found an open seat on a Southwest flight to New Orleans for the following Sunday afternoon. The next evening, while Holly was loading the dishwasher and the sisters were enjoying wine on the front porch, Mikki broke the news. "I have a Sunday flight to New Orleans."

Sophia turned the wineglass stem with her fingers. "I guessed you'd be leaving soon."

"No more therapy, so no more excuses for sitting around."

"Do you need a ride to the airport?" She didn't have a Symphony commitment that day.

Mikki shook her head. "Hank offered."

Sophia grinned. "Did he now."

"Don't go there. He has to pick his daughters up anyway."

"Ah, well, that explains it."

Older sisters never stopped being a pain.

"You could do worse."

"I have done worse. But I'm not looking for romance. I'm looking for a job. I would like to have some of my life back."

"I know. How do you think your hand will hold up?"

Mikki placed her left hand on her knee. "We'll find out soon enough. Even if it's okay, a lot of people in the business know what happened and might think I'm too great a risk."

"True."

"Have you heard whether you're getting the Principal job?"

"Yes I have, and yes I did."

Mikki reached between their chairs to touch her arm. "Oh wow, great, but you haven't mentioned anything." Then she got it. "Oh."

"Yeah, *Oh*. I haven't told them yet."

Mikki could fill in the blanks.

Hank Duncan almost never acted on impulse. Most of his life choices had been approached rationally. Even marrying Taylor had, at the time, seemed rational; she was smart, ambitious and—oh yes—hot. They had dated a couple of months before Hank used the word *girlfriend*, another year before they got married. And since the divorce, he had only been serious about one other woman, Josie, the soccer coach at the high school. They'd been dating two years when she announced she was going on a year's exchange coaching job in Ireland. She was still there.

Why was he attracted to women who, at some point in the relationship, chose jobs over him?

And here he was again. Interested in a high profile musician trying to find an equally high profile job—some place other than Colorado. He clearly had a type. And it wasn't a woman who wanted to iron his shirts and cook his meals.

Just before noon Sunday, he sat in his car in the Perillo driveway, watching Mikki say goodbye to her sister and niece, reminding himself that she would probably not be back. There was nothing for her here. And until his girls graduated, he wasn't going anywhere. Cate and Erin had already had one major life-change. Evergreen was providing stability. Based on her past, Mikki would probably not choose or enjoy stability.

During the drive to the airport, their conversation included the weather: what it would be like in New Orleans, certainly not like the blustery day Denver was having. Her trip: "How long is the flight?"

"Two and half hours, plus the time zone change."

"Is your friend Noah meeting you?"

"No, the group he's with performs weekend nights. He mailed me the spare key to his apartment. Noah's not done till midnight."

"When you get a job, will you let me know? And about your hand." She nodded.

Hank was negotiating the roads and signs heading into Denver International, finally stopping in the East Terminal loading zone. He turned the engine off and got out to lift her suitcase from the back, setting it on the sidewalk and pulling up the handle.

As he turned around, she was conveniently beside him so he pulled her into his arms and kissed her. Once. Twice. Before he got to three, she moved away hesitantly.

A little unsteady, "Thanks for everything."

Somehow, *you're welcome* didn't fit the moment.

"Take care." He leaned over to kiss her cheek, then watched her walk into the terminal.

When he arrived at Taylor's, he pulled into the loading zone and texted Cate: **I'm downstairs.** He didn't want to deal with his ex—not today when his thoughts were on Mikki and what had ended even before it got started.

9

No messages from Mikki.

Sophia wasn't surprised. Her sister had never been one to share the details of her life but, after Mikki had lived in Evergreen for three plus months, Sophia hoped for at least an **I'm OK** or **I found work** on her phone. She sent Mikki several **How is New Orleans? Are you working?** texts. Silence. Holly reported that Erin's father was also wondering whether Mikki had surfaced. Clearly, Sophia wasn't the only one being ignored.

At the moment, Sophia was dealing with Dante's prickly reaction to her accepting the new Symphony job without running it by him first.

"What will this job entail? How much more of your time will it take?" No *Congratulations on the promotion.* Just interrogation.

"I don't know yet. But there's a raise attached."

"Did you think about how this will affect Holly's routine?"

Of course she had.

Sophia was tempted to point out Holly's routine hadn't been his priority for a long time, but that truth could ignite open warfare. The hidden warfare they were conducting was already taking enough of a toll on the whole family.

"I have the name of an experienced, well-recommended high school senior who drives and is very responsible. Her name is Ashley. My raise should cover her salary. I'm hoping I'll only need her twice a week. Some weeks not at all."

Pushing his cup aside. "I want to meet her before you finalize all of this."

"Of course." Sophia suspected that underneath his harshness, he was actually relieved he would not have to be home for Holly.

Dante stood up and set his empty coffee cup in the sink. "I'm expecting a lumber delivery," and left the kitchen.

Sophia stayed at the table, staring at nothing. Though she was glad she'd finally told him, she couldn't figure out why he was so angry about family-related responsibilities.

I want!

Really?

They used to enjoy each other's company. Cooking together, quiet conversations after Holly was in bed. There was no laughter anymore. And it wasn't because Mikki had been staying with them. The attitude change had begun before her arrival.

The only email message Mikki responded to came from Ardith the week after Thanksgiving. Afraid something might have happened to her father, she opened it and found the attachment announcing Jon and Ardith's marriage. Over the four-day holiday, they had flown to Las Vegas and finally tied the knot.

The morning after Mikki opened the announcement, Jon called Sophia. "She's at least alive. Ardith set a trigger on the server to show the sender that the email message had been opened. School counselors use those settings to make sure students can't say **I didn't receive the message.**"

"But it can't tell us where Mikki is."

"No. We'd have to bug her phone to do that. Imagine how mad she'd be if we did. She has never dealt well with people interfering in her life."

"What's your guess about the job hunt and her hand?"

"Probably not as good as Mikki would like. Thus the silence. How are things at your house?"

She sighed. "We don't have enough time to go there. Tell Ardith hello."

Dumping on her father wasn't worthwhile at this point. Holly was flourishing. She loved her fifth grade teacher, had become BFF's with Erin Duncan, and was adjusting to Ashley being part of her life. Sophia's new job, however, came with something of a learning curve, some of the work involving personnel issues as well as music. Immersed in Perillo Woods, Dante had forgotten their anniversary and still had not attended any of Holly's soccer games. Sophia might as well be a single parent.

Mikki had seldom failed to achieve any goal she set her mind to: She earned a spot in the Front Range Young Artists Piano Recital when she was eleven, outperforming the older students. Several times during high school, she was invited as guest soloist with the Denver Youth Orchestra. After graduating with honors from high school, she received a full-ride music scholarship to Northwestern. However, the most important honor was Jay recruiting her for *Gaining Ground*.

More than once, Sophia had complained—at some length—that her younger sister had an unfair number of musical opportunities dropped into her lap. Case in point, her years in *Gaining Ground*.

Since the crash however, nothing was falling into Mikki's lap. After two months of failing to find a high profile gig in New Orleans, she was depressed and not particularly grateful for the Monday through Friday job that Noah had found in Sorrentos, a small Italian restaurant off, off, off Bourbon Street. She definitely did not want to discuss her failure with her family or Hank via phone texts. It was hard enough to talk to Noah, who had been brilliant through it all.

When she arrived in September, he had already arranged for her to have access to the piano in Jazz City, *Upbeat's* current venue, before it opened for the lunch crowd. He also canvassed the New Orleans music scene and found her three auditions during October. The first with a trio that did weddings, bar mitzvahs and the like. Unfortunately, they felt her style was too aggressive for their clientele. Aggressive, really? Strike one. The second was *The Ragin' Cajuns*, a band with a sound similar to Jay's; it was on the cusp of a US tour. They said *no* because they were concerned about her hand, afraid of having to replace her during the tour. The third strike came from a five-piece group that loved her sound but decided to go with the nephew of the band's stage manager.

The rejections hurt. Noah's reminder that rejection was a reality in the music business did not help.

For the moment, she was breaking even financially. Noah had refused her offer to split the rent, suggesting she keep the refrigerator stocked instead. She was pretty sure her living with him was not doing his love life any good, but he didn't complain. There was, however, the possibility that having Mikki as his roommate was protecting Noah from girlfriends wanting to move in. An unofficial gatekeeper.

All of the above were minor annoyances in comparison with the conundrum running a continuous loop through her head: If this is all there is of her career, then who is Mikki Richards if she can't be Mikki Richards, jazz pianist? From the day she arrived at Northwestern, it had never occurred to her she would not be a working musician. Playing for the dinner crowd at a neighborhood restaurant was humiliating.

Giving piano lessons to bored seven year olds would be embarrassing. *Those who can do, those who can't*—etc.

Having left her car in Evergreen, walking New Orleans was both a necessity and a way of learning the city, letting the kaleidoscope of colors and designs envelop her. Layers and layers of balconies embroidered with wrought iron artwork, the architectural signature of the French Quarter. On Bourbon Street, rows of glass-paned doors opened out onto the sidewalks, creating a fluid inside/outside ambiance. Some clubs had pitchmen stationed at the doors, encouraging pedestrians to come inside. A carnival-like energy. The myriad colors and sounds were even more compelling at night and, since she didn't have anything else to do, she often walked among the tourists enjoying the celebratory atmosphere.

The day Jazz City was putting up Christmas decorations, Mikki's morning practice session was cut short. She begged coffee from the bar, tucked herself into a booth, and laid out the pages with Jay's notes. In a desperate attempt to remind herself of happier days, she'd resurrected one of her compositions that Teri found in Jay's baggage after the crash. She was reworking the beginning, adjusting the rhythm to get the piece off to a brighter start. And simplifying the bass clef without losing the original sound.

The discipline of daily practice was the best part of her day. Dressed in denim leggings, a sweatshirt, and running shoes, her hair once again long enough for a ponytail, she'd walked the four blocks from the streetcar stop on Canal to the club on Bourbon. She was learning that two hours of playing necessitated two Advil tablets before she began. Hopefully, playing would get easier. Had to. Each morning she ran scales, played some of *Gaining Ground's* repertoire.

Even though he'd arranged for the practice space and her job, Noah was worried that she was pushing her hand too much. He wanted her to cut back to one practice hour in the morning. So far she was getting by with only two pills a day. But she'd gone back to wearing the brace unless she was playing. Her evening gig didn't put as much stress on her hand as practicing did. To add variety to the Sorrentos' performances, she was experimenting with talk/singing lyrics to some of the pieces. She didn't have much range, but she could stay on key and no one had complained.

Since his divorce, Hank was accustomed to sharing the girls with Taylor at Christmas. This year, they spent Christmas Eve with him and Grace, and Christmas day with Taylor. As soon as he returned from delivering them to Denver on Christmas morning, he went out to Grace's. She always cooked a ham dinner for him and anyone she knew who would otherwise be alone on the holiday. Sometimes there were six or seven friends, sometimes just the two of them. This year, Manny and his wife Tina came for dinner, contributing a baking dish piled with homemade tamales. They left Grace's just before five o'clock to visit Tina's mother in a memory care facility in Denver, leaving Grace and Hank to clean up and face the usual letdown that followed the holiday.

While Grace put leftovers in storage containers, Hank loaded the dishwasher and dealt with the pots and pans. He looked around, "Is that everything?"

"Close enough." Grace put the last container in the refrigerator. "Do you have time for wine?"

"Always."

The 50's style fireplace in the wood-paneled living room gave the appearance of warmth without really providing any. Hank turned the furnace thermostat up a few degrees to defend against the dropping temperature outside. Snow was predicted for tomorrow. Grace brought two wine glasses, handing one to Hank and settling herself into the upholstered rocker that had been her seat-of-choice for years. Whenever the fabric wore out, she had it reupholstered. Hank sat on the couch, leaning forward, his elbows on his knees as though he didn't want to get too comfortable.

"I talked to Sophia; she gave me the phone number and address for Mikki's friend Noah. Also the name of the restaurant where Mikki is playing during the week. Sophia suggested that I not call ahead. Surprise might be wiser."

"Remind me. When do you leave? I wrote it down but then erased it from my memory."

"January 4th. The conference begins on the 5th, ends the 9th. I'll drive to New Orleans the next day and figure out where to stay once I get there."

"And you're doing this because?"

"You know perfectly well why." A carefully defensive tone.

She laughed. "But it's my great pleasure to give you a hard time."

"Umm. Well, I may end up with egg on my face."

"Wouldn't be the first time. I'm glad you're getting out of town and glad you like Mikki. The girls and I will be fine. I haven't seen much of them since Taylor's been back in the neighborhood." She would be staying in Hank's house rather than moving the girls to hers.

"Just don't let Cate talk you into too much driving."

"I might be old but I'm not easy."

"No one would ever accuse you of that." He said it with a smile. During his childhood, she had been the family disciplinarian, his dad the soft place to fall.

Hank hadn't expected to miss Mikki as much as he did. After all, she'd only been his patient for a few months. During his years at the clinic, hundreds of patients had come and gone. While he was their therapist, he cared about their recovery, but the caring ended there. However, a little at a time, Mikki had become more than a patient, an entirely different kind of caring. An intriguing, courageous, sexy woman that he wanted to know better. Not until he kissed her the day they went to Georgetown did he realize he'd been wanting to do that for a while.

He didn't normally attend the yearly American Physical Therapy Conference, but Houston's proximity to New Orleans was too convenient to ignore. He wanted to see her. Figure out whether he was making more of the kiss and his feelings than he should. And so he asked his mother to kid-sit, and Grace, being Grace, asked searching questions he couldn't escape.

Though music, especially jazz, was everywhere in New Orleans, Mikki was still on the outside looking in. When she first arrived, she'd gone to Jazz City a few times to listen to Noah's new band, to immerse herself in the atmosphere. Imagine herself on that stage. It didn't take her long to admit she wasn't part of any of it, so she stopped going.

She found herself suspended between the world that *Gaining Ground* had provided and five nights a week in a somewhat ordinary restaurant where people came for the food, not the music. Frustration didn't begin to describe her feelings. And to top it off, Noah suddenly accepted a new job with an LA band, *Tangerine Slices*. He would leave in early January, just before *Gaining Ground's* album of their Rome performance was released.

If Mikki stayed in New Orleans, she'd need to figure out how to pay the rent, find a smaller place or get a roommate. But staying would just perpetuate her situation. And she couldn't keep following Noah. Especially since his newest girlfriend, Caron something or other, was going with him.

Mikki was on her own. No network, a few casual friends. And her hand, though stronger, was still not 100%.

The Thursday that Noah left for LA, Mikki almost called the restaurant to tell them she was too sick to come in. But she wasn't sick—just bummed—and she needed the money. The rent was paid until the end of the month. Her car was at Sophia's, her modest amount of furniture in Chicago and, according to an email from her father, he would be spending the spring and summer teaching graduate level workshops at the U of New Hampshire. Ardith was taking leave from her high school job. **You know where the house key is.** Mikki might just have to take him up on it. She certainly couldn't impose on Sophia again. Everything kept changing like chess pieces on a board.

So at 5:30 on a Friday night, she was sitting at the **Employees only** table next to the kitchen, fortifying herself with lasagna, salad, and wine while she worked out which pieces she was going to use that evening. She was embarrassed that she had reverted to using sheet music. Her ability to memorize—absorb— music had always left her free to improvise, to run with whatever the band members were doing. But somewhere in the last months, she'd lost the ability to play her old repertoire from memory, and the need to follow the notes on a page interfered with the quality of her playing. It was like a faucet had turned off. Noah had been as puzzled about the change as she was. Certainly her memory was not connected to her left hand.

10

The PT conference, like most professional gatherings, started strong and after three days lost steam. Too late, Hank remembered why he rarely attended. On Friday morning, he rented an economy car, checked out of the hotel a day early, and made the five-hour drive to New Orleans. The flatness of the Gulf Coast and its immense distances were startling to a man who lived surrounded by perpendicular mountains. He let his mind wander. No need to focus yet. He didn't have a game plan. Simply to see that she was okay.

Mikki saw Hank when she returned from her dinner break. He was seated at a small table along the windows adjacent to the street, giving his order to Ruben, one of the owner's many relatives. She made herself concentrate on the music in front of her, pretending he wasn't there because she wasn't sure how she felt about his being there.

Since the piano was behind him, Hank heard the music before he saw Mikki. She was intent on the pages stretched across the music rack, the melody quietly sliding beneath the cacophony of the dining room. And then she was singing along. Almost as though she were alone, singing to herself. Her voice was low, husky, not presenting the words as a performance, allowing them to blend into the music. Her playing was quieter, not the energetic, chord-driven jazz that she'd played in Rome.

He turned his chair so he was looking at her, wondering how long it would take her to notice him. She was wearing a filmy long skirt ablaze with colors and a matching sleeveless top. A rather bohemian look. Her hair was below her shoulders, much longer than when he'd last seen her. When that piece ended, she segued into another without waiting for applause. It wasn't an applause kind of venue. Because he was so intent on watching her, he was surprised when his meal arrived. Reluctantly, he turned his chair around so he could do justice to the steaming lasagna and arugula side salad.

He was lingering over his second glass of wine when Mikki stopped alongside his table. "Do you mind if I join you?" The words hesitant.

"Please do. You're the reason I'm here."

A nice line. She slid into the chair opposite him.

"Would you like some wine?"

"Absolutely. I ran out of water half an hour ago."

He motioned to Ruben, pointed to Mikki, then to his glass. Ruben headed for the bar but didn't bring her the same wine Hank had. He knew her preference.

Unsure what Hank's being here meant, she chose a safe question, "When did you get here?"

"Here, here? Or New Orleans?"

"Both."

"Here—eight o'clock. You were on a break. New Orleans, this afternoon about one o'clock." Pointing at her brace. "You're still using it?"

She nodded. "I cut out an hour of practice time in the mornings and went back to using this when I'm not playing so I could get rid of the pain pills."

"Good choice." He waited. "So how do you like New Orleans?"

She shrugged. "I don't know much about it. Don't know all that many people." She paused, "Noah left for Los Angeles yesterday."

"Permanently?"

"As permanent as playing in a band ever is." She'd learned that the hard way.

Not sure what Noah and Mikki's relationship was now, Hank didn't ask whether she'd thought of going with him. But he was relieved she hadn't.

"I'm guessing my sister sold me out."

"No money changed hands—but yes, she did. Neither she nor your father could get away, and I was going to Houston, so—"

"What was in Houston?"

"A tedious, sometimes informative convention that I skipped out on today."

"To come here."

He smiled slightly, "To come here."

"To see me."

"To see you." He was rather enjoying the banter. Another reason he'd missed her.

"And now that you've seen me?"

Hank debated his response—deciding to stay in banter mode. "You look different. I like it."

"It's actually an old look, my performance look. Except I didn't go back to blonde streaks. Too much trouble and money."

He finished his wine. "Since your car is still at your sister's, would you like a ride home?"

"Yes. That would be nice. The streetcars only run once an hour at night. I actually don't mind using public transportation. I like the anonymity of it."

As they rounded the corner onto Camp Street, she pointed ahead. "The gray building with the blue trim. The curb is painted as a loading zone."

Hank parked and turned the engine off. Now the ever-awkward moment between genders. He didn't want to presume too much—risk messing things up. "Are you busy tomorrow? Since I have the car until I leave Sunday, we might do the tourist thing. I've never been here before. Do you work tomorrow night?"

"No, not on weekends."

"How about I pick you up around 10?"

"Okay. Text me and I'll come down. It's easier. Thanks for the ride."
And just like that, she exited the car and was halfway up the stairs of the
building before Hank could say anything else.

Awkwardness avoided—or just delayed.

With the help of the tourist map he purchased at the hotel gift shop,
he spent the rest of the evening deciding on an itinerary that would
also allow conversation. This wasn't really about the city. It was about
spending time with her.

Saturday morning, he returned to the same curb, texted her and,
when she'd settled into the passenger seat, handed her take-out coffee.
"Good morning. I hope it's still hot."

"Where's yours?"

"I drank it on the way over, couldn't resist the aroma."

Mikki sipped hers. "Strong and hot."

"Too strong? I guessed at how much cream. I knew you didn't take
sugar."

He'd paid attention. "Just right."

He handed her the street map. "I thought we'd start at Jackson
Square."

Good coffee and sunshine. Mikki relaxed into the day.

Based on their afternoon in Georgetown, Hank assumed Mikki was
a wanderer, not needing to go into museums or take a city bus tour while
someone with a microphone rattled off easily forgotten historical details
and told bad jokes. When Hank traveled—which wasn't very often—he
preferred to see with his feet. Walking gave an up-close-and-personal
view. From Jackson Square, they strolled the side streets, stopping
to admire a garden or comment on the rainbow-colored houses. She
didn't chatter; he liked that. She listened and responded. He'd wanted
conversation and she was doing her part. Though she'd traveled to places

he'd only heard about, she didn't draw comparisons. Didn't say, *"When I was in—"*

They circled back to Jackson Square, bought drinks and sandwiches at a deli, and found an outside table. They took time to watch the artists working around the cathedral's perimeter, then went into the church for a few minutes.

Though Mikki had explored much of the Quarter after her practice sessions, she was seeing it differently, through his eyes. She discovered he liked the bold colors of the houses and knew the names of many of the flowers in the yards. Probably Grace's influence. The best part, she didn't have to work at making conversation. Like the day in Georgetown, they did silence comfortably.

There was no touching, though there was a sense of touching, more tantalizing than if he had taken her hand.

After lunch, instead of more walking, they drove across the Lake Pontchartrain Causeway to Mandeville, indulged in ice cream cones and sat on a bench, looking across the shallow lake. Mikki realized she hadn't once thought about music, her hand, or what she was going to do now that Noah was gone. Remarkable to just be in the moment. Enjoying the day. And Hank's company.

"Are you free for dinner?"

"Yes."

"Have you been to Antoine's?"

"No, but I've certainly heard of it."

"Just in case you might want to go, I had the hotel concierge make a reservation for tonight, seven o'clock."

"Sounds good."

Even though he'd arrived in New Orleans without a specific plan, the day had been close to perfect. Antoine's was a tradition in New Orleans. A French-Creole menu, formal dining room, ceiling fans, mirrored walls, and white tablecloths preserved its Nineteenth Century heritage. Simple and elegant. As they read the menu, Hank and Mikki caught themselves talking in hushed tones usually reserved for churches and art museums.

They decided to share the Oysters Rockefeller appetizer. Neither had ever tried them. Hank predictably chose the steak entrée, which came with a vegetable. Mikki chose the shrimp entrée and salad. They let the waiter choose the wine and delayed a decision on dessert.

When the waiter left, Mikki admitted, "Not as expensive as I would have thought." She'd never lost the habit of reading the right side of the menu.

"Agreed." He smiled.

She smiled back.

They took their time over the food, savoring every morsel, commenting on the other patrons, watching the waiters in their formal black suits performing their duties—a kind of choreographed dance. Pouring the wine, setting each plate in front of a customer with a flourish—as though no food had ever been so remarkable.

They skipped dessert, finishing the last of the wine. Hank was telling a story about Erin and Holly at the Evergreen ice rink. "They talked some of the other kids into playing crack the whip, which is risky on an empty pond but on the town rink, a definite no-no. They're banned for the rest of the winter."

"I bet it was Holly's idea. She knows no fear when it comes to things like that. Does she know you're in New Orleans?"

"Maybe." He thought about his next words, hesitated, then jumped off a cliff. "Are you going to stay here, now that Noah's gone?" He'd been wanting to ask all day.

As she twisted the stem of the wine glass, he could feel her tense up. "There isn't much for me here."

"Where would you go?" He doubted Evergreen was high on the list.

Mikki shrugged slightly, not wanting to talk about the fear that was sitting on her heart. Today had been so wonderful. Now he'd spoiled it.

She could feel her neck and shoulders tightening. She avoided looking at him directly.

"Sorry, I shouldn't have—"

"I don't have an answer." She spread her left hand on the table. Long fingers, short, unpolished nails, no rings. She'd left the brace at the apartment for the evening. "My hand works but not as well as it did. People who make hiring decisions don't want to take a chance. What I'm doing now doesn't hurt my hand but doesn't pay enough."

"Are there other ways to earn a living as a musician?" He knew he'd phrased that badly.

She pushed the empty glass away. "Sure. I can teach," she looked at him intently, "but I don't want to teach. It's like saying you're washed up, put out to pasture. Before I was 30, I was part of something bigger and better. I got used to the lifestyle, the excitement of performing. Maybe the attention. I don't want to listen to badly done scales and deal with demanding parents." Mikki could feel her emotions interfering. "I'm tired. I'd like to go home."

Hank signaled the waiter. This wasn't the way he hoped the evening would go. He doubted they were at the stay all night stage, but he'd wanted to open a door that they could revisit. He'd screwed up. Asked about what she was still processing. He'd underestimated the trauma of her lost dream. When he'd lost his, he still had the girls. She didn't have anything else to anchor her.

They rode to her place, trapped in the wrong kind of silence. The softness, closeness of the day replaced by her distress. Once again he parked at the curb in front of the gray apartment building.

"Thanks for today. I'll remember it." Again she fled the car, unlocking the door to the lobby before he could reach her. He was left standing beside the car, looking and feeling like a fool.

When Hank got home mid-afternoon on Sunday, the house was empty, a note from his mother on the kitchen table: **At the movies. We'll bring pizza**.

Just as well. He wasn't ready to unpack the details of his week with anyone, especially his family. Though he realized he hadn't done anything terrible, he had definitely misjudged Mikki's state of mind. Trained since childhood to move on when things didn't work out, he'd assumed that, by now, Mikki would have thought about what might come next. He was just beginning to admit he wanted to be part of whatever that would be.

He kept remembering kissing her and Mikki kissing back. He had, however, poured cold water on whatever beginnings of a relationship there were, with no clue how to fix it. The male penchant for fixing things rarely worked when the problem was wrapped up in emotion. He should have walked more carefully. He and Taylor had tried to fix their marriage and that hadn't worked.

The girls were in high spirits when they got home. Going to the movies was always a treat—so was take out. They'd chosen a large pizza with three toppings. To prove he'd done tourist things while he was gone, he'd snapped a few pictures of the colorful New Orleans houses and gardens. One of Antoine's. One of Mikki with her ice cream cone, a triple-decker: Strawberry, Chocolate and Pistachio. In between pictures, he managed to superficially explain what Mikki was doing without giving his personal disappointment away. These days, Erin and Holly told each other everything. Sophia didn't need to hear about Mikki's emotional state from her daughter. When the girls had gone to their rooms, Grace fixed the mother-eye on him.

"And Mikki?"

"Good and not-so-good. Her hand is gradually improving, but she's not in a good place mentally." He reached for the last sliver of pizza.

"And?"

"And until I asked what she was going to do next, it was a great day. But once that topic came up, the walls also came up."

Grace waited a few minutes. When he didn't continue, she picked up the small canvas duffle bag she used whenever she stayed over. "I've got an early delivery." She touched his shoulder as she passed him. "Don't beat up on yourself; I'll let myself out."

Once the need to be sociable was gone, he headed for the shower. It had been a long day. Two hours at the New Orleans airport, two plus hours in the air, topped off with the drive from Denver to Evergreen.

He was grateful for plenty of hot water and the clean sheets on his bed.

Though Mikki had enough money on hand to pay another month's rent, sinking more money and time into New Orleans would be counterproductive. No sense kidding herself. New Orleans wasn't in need of her talent or what was left of it. She gave the building manager and the furniture rental company two weeks notice, then did the same at the restaurant. Decisions that felt like stepping into empty air. This time Noah wasn't around to pick up the pieces. At a subconscious level, she knew—but didn't want to know—that she needed to sort the situation out by herself. She was definitely embarrassed about her reaction to Hank's question. Saturday had been an enjoyable day—until she stomped all over it. She liked him, hadn't really intended to shoot down whatever was almost tangible between them. But she had.

Two days later, Teri's email offered a detour: **The Rome album will be on the market next week. Can you come before next Wednesday? I'm scheduled for Chicago AM on WGN. Come hold my hand. My spare room is vacant—no more drummer boy.**

Okay.

Mikki had been toying with the idea of finding out how many units she needed to finish her bachelor's degree. An in-person visit to Northwestern would be more effective than trying to sort out her records on-line. Perhaps Teri's invitation was part of the answer to what came next. She booked a seat on a Tuesday flight and packed what few belongings she had with her. No one to say goodbye to, probably no one would notice her absence.

The ever-present pity party showed up again.

One of the constants of Mikki's relationship with Teri was that, even when they hadn't seen one another for many months, they could pick up where they had left off, as though no time had elapsed. This time was no different, except that Teri had lost weight and looked sleep deprived. When Mikki commented, Teri replied with, "It's called a break-up diet. The stress strips the pounds right off."

They were eating take-out Chinese straight from the containers, sitting in front of Teri's gas-fed fireplace. The condo was on the tenth floor of a high rise overlooking Lake Michigan. Definitely posh.

"When did it happen?" Mikki was pretty sure she knew why.

"When I made the mistake of picking up his iPhone instead of mine and finding messages and x-rated pictures from someone named Wendy. When I confronted him, he couldn't very well deny what was on his phone. Though for a hot minute he tried."

"Are you going to be okay?"

"Jury's still out, but probably." She didn't sound convinced. "What about you? Anyone on your horizon? I hope you and Noah didn't change your friendship status."

"Safe there. His latest conquest followed him to LA." Mikki wasn't sure she wanted to wade into the Hank situation, then did. "My physical therapist came to see me in New Orleans last week. We spent a really nice day together, but I screwed up. So the answer is no one on the horizon."

"What's he like?"

Mikki reached for a fortune cookie, broke it open, and laughed. "Who thinks these up?" She laid the tiny strip of paper on the table. "He's divorced, has custody of his two daughters, one is 15, the other is almost 11. Late thirties, intense brown eyes. Low key, kind."

"Beats drummers who are always on the prowl."

"He's a partner in the clinic I was assigned to, and I doubt he's going anywhere while his girls are in school. He lives in a stable world, except for ex-wife issues."

"And you're not used to stable. Have you slept together?" Teri was not given to tiptoeing around topics.

"Didn't get that far." Time to change the subject. "What about the album?"

Teri handed Mikki a CD from the stack on the coffee table. "So much is online and downloaded into phones these days that CD's seem old fashioned."

The cover showed the band in Rome. Mikki felt tears prick at her eyes. The CD was titled **Finale.**

"Want me to play it?"

"Not if you want me to stay dry-eyed."

"Yeah. It's hard to listen to."

"Is this the end of your work for the band?"

Teri nodded.

"What's next?" This time she got to ask the question.

"Next week, my sister and I are going to Maui for ten days. No idea about work. This was a high-pressure job, and I'm not sure I want to get back into that kind of rat race. Jay set me up with a small bequest to tide me over for a bit. And you?"

"A little cash from selling my condo. Not sure I want to be on the road again with another band, even if they'd have me. Jay was one of a kind. But I really do miss the excitement of performing." She paused. She hadn't told anyone else this. "I'm going to talk to Northwestern about finishing my degree. I was within a few units of graduating. But some of the units might have vaporized." She took her empty carton into the kitchen. "What time is your interview?"

"We need to be at the station by 6:30."

Mikki groaned. "Make sure I've heard my alarm."

Teri didn't really need Mikki's help during the ten-minute interview at WGN; she'd been doing promos for the band for years. When Teri had answered all the host's questions, Mikki was asked where she was currently performing. Uneasy, she fell back on "My hand is still healing," rather than admit she had nothing to report.

Two days after the CD's release, Teri took off for Hawaii and Mikki stayed in the condo while she coped with the red tape at Northwestern's campus. She waited in lines, waited outside offices and, a week later, was once again a student. Most of her units were still valid. She only needed four units to complete her degree. After three meetings with the Dean of the Music Department, she was offered an Independent Study, using her own compositions, making band arrangements for them. Her association with Jay and the university's pride in his work, helped get her closer to graduation. She had six months to complete the work.

She needed to find someplace to stay or rent. Until the crash, Mikki didn't mind being rootless but, being rootless without the band, was more like being homeless—relying on the kindness of friends and family to keep her from living on the street or in her car. She'd gone from Sophia to Noah to Teri.

For the moment, Greeley looked like the most practical option.

Ardith Richards' house on Fiftieth Street was part of her divorce settlement nine years before she and Jon Richards married. A three-bedroom, white frame and brick bungalow. Unremarkable, except for an elaborate garden watched over by a gardener that came once a week in the summer. The hard Colorado winter did not require a gardener. Once the airport shuttle drove away, it took Mikki only a few minutes to locate the key buried in the flowerbed, currently without flowers, alongside the garage.

Once inside, the first thing she did was turn up the thermostat. Until the temperature got closer to seventy, she'd have to keep her coat on. She needed food. Probably Chinese take out—again.

12

Sophia was waiting outside Holly's school when Mikki's text showed up on her phone: **I'm at Dad's. Is there a time that you could detour from Denver and pick me up so I can retrieve my car?**

And just like that, Mikki was back on the radar. No preamble. No explanation.

Again in need of help. This time, Sophia wasn't in a receptive mood. **Not really.**

It had been a rough couple of months, and now Dante was off buying some exotic wood in Georgia. She felt guilty for refusing but not guilty enough to pick Mikki up, even though getting her car out of the driveway would be a plus.

At that moment, the gates enclosing the school grounds slid open and students raced in all directions. Holly opened the back door, threw her backpack on the car seat, and got in beside her mother. Her ten-year old energy filling the car. "I need to take cookies on Friday for Carmen's birthday party. And not store-bought ones."

It was time to start teaching Holly to bake. Unfortunately, it was simpler for Sophia to make them herself. Cookies and Dante and her job and Mikki were competing for her time and attention. When did she get to take a trip to Georgia or anywhere?

By the time she pulled into her driveway, she'd worked out a solution for the car retrieval problem. When she'd given Hank Duncan Mikki's contact information in New Orleans, he'd thanked her with "I owe you."

Time to collect.

On Mikki's first day in Greeley, the three-block walk to the Safeway made it clear she needed her car. Walking wasn't the issue, carrying the groceries was. How did people without cars manage? Icy sidewalks were an additional hazard.

Sophia's **Not Really** answer about the car was unhelpful to say the least. But Mikki guessed she'd asked for help one time too many. She'd have to check what Uber or Lyft would charge for a trip to Evergreen. She also needed to let her father know that she was staying at the house—ask if there were things she needed to know about water pipes or the heater? And soon she needed to lay out a schedule for arranging the music she owed Northwestern. Fortunately, Ardith had a console piano, not the instrument Mikki preferred but she was grateful she wouldn't have to rent one. She didn't know whether Ardith played because Mikki had been with *Gaining Ground* when Jon and Ardith became a couple. Whatever was going on with the band had always been more important to Mikki than whatever was going on in her family. Being a professional musician was more interesting, definitely more glamorous. In those years, it hadn't occurred to her that she might have to confront ordinary tasks in the everyday world. Or ask her family for help.

A little after ten on Saturday, the doorbell interrupted her Uber price check. Probably a high school student selling something she didn't want. She opened the door and found Hank on the doorstep with two cups of coffee in a carry carton. "I brought coffee." He smiled.

Her surprise momentarily stole her speech.

"I realize you weren't expecting me but, since it's cold out here, may I come in? The coffee's getting cold."

"Ah, um of course. Sorry." She moved aside so he could enter. He handed her the cup that had a large M on the side. "I don't mean to be ungracious but why—"

"—am I here?" He finished her sentence.

"Yeah. I've only been here three days."

"Your sister reminded me that I owed her a favor."

"And I'm payback?"

"Sort of. You need a ride to Evergreen, and I'm going back there as soon as you're ready."

Mikki finally put the pieces together. "You dropped your girls off in Denver."

"Correct. Sophia suggested I make a side trip to Greeley." He took a sip of his coffee. "Where should I wait?"

"Living room, I guess." She pointed to the room on her left. "I won't be long."

Once in the guest room, she wasn't sure what to do first, how much to do. She pulled off the old fleece she was wearing, then slipped a rather expensive yellow sweater over her head. In the bathroom, she washed her face, put on a little makeup, nothing too obvious, and brushed her hair, reminding herself she needed a trim.

She instinctively wanted to look good. For him. She wasn't sure whether she should be embarrassed by her cliché behavior or not.

By the time she had the coffee cup back in her hand, the coffee was tepid, but she drank it anyway. She needed something besides Hank to concentrate on. He didn't say anything until they were on I-70, exiting Denver. Then a question from left field, "Did you grow up in Greeley?"

"We moved there when I was four. My father had just finished his Doctorate in Laramie. He's been at Northern Colorado ever since."

"Where is he now?"

"In New Hampshire, giving a series of financial workshops for MBA candidates."

"Ah the financial world. He and Taylor would find plenty to talk about."

"Probably."

"What does your stepmother do?"

"She's a counselor at Northridge High School."

"Do you like her?"

Mikki shrugged. "Don't know her very well, but I'm grateful she doesn't mind my staying in her house, their house, for a while." Mikki didn't want to open up the *What comes next* topic again, so she asked "How are your daughters?"

"Do you want the long or short version?"

"Short."

"Well, Erin and Holly took on the manager at the ice rink and groveled enough to be allowed back. They are a formidable combination. Cate likes someone named Mitch in her Physics class and is hoping he'll ask her to the next dance. The only thing her mother and I agree on is no steady boyfriend until she's a senior, and maybe not even then. Every week there's a new issue."

For the remainder of the trip, conversation sputtered. Each of them being cautious, remembering what happened in New Orleans. Just outside Evergreen, it began to drizzle, not quite cold enough for snow. Time to say something.

"What do you do with yourself when Erin and Cate are in Denver?"

"Well, there's always laundry and grocery shopping. No yard work in the winter unless there's snow to shovel. Our cleaning lady, Mrs. Nevins, was here Wednesday so not much cleaning required for a day or two."

As he pulled into the Perillo driveway, Mikki undid her seatbelt. "Thanks for the ride."

Before it was too late, he asked. "Do you ski?"

"I'm from Colorado, skiing is required. I haven't been on the slopes for a couple of years. Probably a bit rusty."

Holly had come out onto the front porch, watching them.

"The girls will be at Taylor's over the President's Day holiday, maybe on that Sunday you can come to my place, and we'll go to Echo Mountain. It's close and not as busy as resorts like Breckenridge or Keystone."

She didn't hesitate—a good sign— "Sure. I'd like that." She turned to look at him, the hint of a smile in her eyes.

"Good. I'll get lift tickets on line."

"What time?"

"Ten?"

"Okay. Thanks again for the ride." She opened the door. "Let me know if something changes."

He nodded and shifted into reverse.

When she and Holly finished hugging, "Where's your mother."

"Practicing."

"How long?"

"An hour so far."

"She needs a break. Let me talk to her alone. Okay?" Mikki was certain Sophia would not be happy with her. No sense subjecting Holly to a sister tangle. Interrupting Sophia's practice time was always risky, but Mikki wanted to get back to Greeley in case it began to snow. Her mind was going in a dozen directions at once. She wondered if Ardith had skis she could use. Could the Chicago storage company get her clothing boxes here in time.

She knocked on the door: "Soph, it's me. Can I come in?"

After a few minutes, the door opened, Sophia holding her violin and bow in one hand. An off-putting frown. "The car key is in the drawer where I keep the plastic lids." No soft edges. Straight to the chase.

"I know; I brought the duplicate just in case."

Sophia moved away from the entrance and returned to the straight-backed chair in front of the music stand, hinting that she wanted to get back to her music.

Mikki closed the door. Otherwise Holly might join them. "Thanks for getting Hank to pick me up."

"I've just been really busy."

"I get it. I've already taken up too much of your life," she said it lightly, but she knew Sophia did not hear lightness because her expression was still borderline angry.

Mikki tried a softer method. "Are you okay, Soph?"

"Just busy." She placed the violin and bow on the low table alongside the music stand. "I didn't appreciate you going off the grid."

"Sorry."

"You've always done that—act like what you do or don't do has no effect on anyone else. Dad was really worried about you, and I got the brunt of him being upset. I don't have time to put out your fires. I have enough fires of my own."

Mikki started to reply but wasn't fast enough. "Nothing at Christmas, no thanks for the gift Holly made you. You were that way when you were a kid. You were the super talented one, so if you had any kind of a problem, everyone jumped to solve it for you so you could concentrate on your music. You never learned to take care of yourself or think about anyone else. You're just so selfish. Well, Marguerite Louise, I have news. You're in your thirties and it's not all about you anymore. It's time you step up and be a part of our world. It's not all applause and fame. And this is not sour grapes talking because I don't live that life." Having made her point, she picked up the violin. "I need to finish."

Mikki knew this was not a time to defend herself, especially since she had no valid defense. She left the room, finding Holly in the hallway, tears threatening.

"Are you and Mom fighting?"

"Not the first time or the last. We'll be okay." *Fingers crossed.*

"She and Dad fight all the time." The tears spilled.

Mikki put her arms around her niece but didn't add more words. Holly needed comfort, not conversation. When Holly was quieter, "Have you had lunch?"

A murmured "No."

"Is there soup?" Mikki excelled at opening cans.

"Tomato, maybe. Can we have cinnamon toast?"

"Sure. You do the toast." Holly liked hers with brown sugar, lots of it, and a minimum amount of cinnamon. "I hear you can go ice skating again."

"We're sort of on probation."

During lunch, Holly brought Mikki up to date on all the things Holly deemed important. It was almost two o'clock, and Sophia was still in her studio. Probably waiting until she heard Mikki's car leave.

Safer that way.

Barricaded in her studio, Sophia wasn't practicing. She was crying—a quiet sort of crying, evidence of pain rather than anger. In truth, she was crying about Dante, afraid that her marriage—wobbly at best—might completely fall apart.

Mikki was a convenient target—but surprisingly she hadn't fought back. It was always too easy to envy Mikki. She had always been determined, seldom failing at anything, not seeming to need anyone. Sophia, on the other hand, needed her family. Losing her mother was a blow to her sense of security. Fortunately, Dante had been there to comfort her, keep her safe from her fears. But now Dante was spending two or three nights a week on the cot in his office, claiming he didn't want to wake her when he came to bed. Their conversations were more and more uncomfortable. She feared Holly would end up like Erin and Cate, shuffled between parents.

As Mikki drove to Greeley, the snow began sticking to the road. For the next week, it snowed on and off so that she had to go looking for her father's snow shovel. At least there would still be good powder for the day of skiing with Hank. She was looking forward to both the skiing and time with him, helping repair what had gone wrong between them. She was surprised by how often she thought about that January day with regret.

Being temporarily settled in Greeley let her relax more than she'd been able to do in New Orleans. She wasn't constantly worrying about her hand, concentrating instead on her compositions. She would need one or two additional pieces. She practiced every morning, worked on writing in the afternoon, and ran errands in between. The car made shopping easier. Snow fell part of every day. As soon as Mikki shoveled the front sidewalk—it acquired another coat of white. As least ice wasn't building up.

She remembered the car probably hadn't been serviced since late summer so she headed for the Ford agency closest to her and ended up spending more than she'd figured on. But without the car, there would be no food or ski trip. She held her breath and gave them her credit card. Thank God for minimum payments.

She contacted the Chicago storage company to have the boxes labeled "clothing" shipped to Greeley. All her winter clothes were in them. She'd been wearing an old down jacket of her father's but had to buy lightweight boots with lug soles. Running shoes did not do snow. She found Ardith's skis suspended from the garage roof, texted her stepmother for permission to use them and got an answer from her father.

Ardith's okay with you borrowing them but what happened to yours?"

Mikki had no answer. Sophia's diatribe kept sneaking into her head. Her sister knew her better than anyone. Since she'd left home, Mikki was responsible only to the band. No one else. She hadn't been much help to her father after her mother's death. A Sophomore at Northwestern., Mikki came home for the funeral and raced back to Chicago, taking refuge in her classes and her music. If no one expects you to show up, it's easy not to show up. Since Sophia had just graduated, she had been the one her father relied on.

She might not have kept track of her skis but, when it came to music, she could transfer into OCD mode. She found the closest Apple store and went for advice on how best to record on her iPhone. She would have to contact Northwestern for help on uploading the recordings when they were finished.

On Sunday morning of Presidents weekend, Hank was watching from his front room window when Mikki's car pulled into his driveway just before ten. His one story, white frame house was on Avon Street in the original part of town. Today the house could be classified as shabby compared to the million dollar structures that had sprouted in the surrounding hills. With current prices off the charts, he probably couldn't afford his own house now, shabby or not. Evergreen had gone upscale and lost some of the small town-ness he'd been drawn to. He'd sunk his share of the Denver house sale into the three-bedroom, one bath structure. There wasn't much front yard, zero lot lines on the sides. A tiny garden in the back. Nothing that required much maintenance.

By the time Mikki got out of her car and began extricating the skis angled across the reclining passenger seat into the back seat, Hank was beside her, helping.

"You found warm clothes."

"My winter clothes arrived from storage yesterday. Just in time, otherwise it would be Levi's, leg warmers, and rented boots. The skis belong to my stepmother." She pulled out the bag holding her ski boots, goggles, gloves and a bottle of water.

Hank was already sliding her skis into the back of his SUV. Ready or not, she was going skiing.

Mikki had forgotten what strenuous exercise combined with cold mountain air could do. She was exhausted in a good way. Ravenous, despite having eaten a huge lunch. Unable to stay awake on the drive back to Evergreen.

It had taken most of the morning to remember how to carve turns, come to a stop, and get on and off the lifts without falling down. She was glad Hank was on the upper, more difficult runs most of the time so she didn't have to embarrass herself. She'd done better in the afternoon, concentrating on putting more pressure on her right ski pole, less on her left.

Around two-thirty, ominous snow clouds began piling up around Mt. Evans. Hank found her on a bench near the intermediate lift. "I think we should get on the road before the snow starts. I hate having to put chains on."

Mikki was grateful for his suggestion. She was running on empty.

When she woke, Hank was pulling into his garage. She straightened in her seat and rubbed her eyes. "Sorry. Just couldn't stay awake."

He shut the engine off. "No worry," he grinned, "you didn't snore. We got here in the nick of time; the snow is beginning to stick to the roads. In another hour, chains will be a must."

Once out of the car, looking at the snow piling up on her car, Mikki realized driving to Denver was probably out of the question. She hadn't wanted to put out the money for snow tires or chains, so now she was effectively grounded.

In Evergreen. At Hank's.

If she and Sophia hadn't just gone three rounds, she could perhaps have bunked at her sister's. But asking would be awkward.

"Come inside. I left the heat on low."

She followed him through the back door into the 1970's kitchen, wood paneling and very little counter space, but at least it was warm. Hank went into the dining room to turn up the thermostat, then came back. "The girls have packages of instant hot chocolate, want some?"

"Are there marshmallows?"

"Sorry. They didn't make it onto the latest grocery list." He took off his down jacket and hung it on one of the hooks by the door.

Mikki wasn't ready to remove hers just yet, processing the fact that her stern physical therapist made grocery lists. He had hidden talents.

By the time they'd finished the hot cocoa, Mikki was warm enough to take her jacket off. Hank had turned on the small TV sitting on the kitchen counter to catch the weather report only to hear the worst words a mountain dweller can hear: **Blizzard conditions from the Wyoming border to Castle Rock.** People were asked to stay off the roads, if possible, so the road crews could work safely. Hank hit mute but left the picture on.

"So, Miss Richards, welcome to Hotel Duncan. There will be no trip to Denver tonight. Or do you want to call your sister?"

She shook her head. "I'm on her shit list right now. Sister issues."

Fortunately, his phone rang so he couldn't ask her to explain. "Hi, Mom." He listened. Listened some more. "Is Manny with you?" More listening. "Okay, we'll be there as soon as we can." He broke the connection. "The heating unit's gone out in the small greenhouse. Everything needs to be transferred to the main one. Want to come?"

After a day on the slopes?

Misreading her hesitancy, "It's okay; Mom knew we were going skiing today."

Before she thought through her response, "Do you tell her everything?"

"Don't have to. Erin is a direct pipeline. She wanted to come with us instead of going to Denver. I need to put my shovel in the car and make sure I have gloves for both of us." He turned down the thermostat, then headed for the garage. "Just close the door. It'll lock."

Mikki stuffed herself back into her jacket and wrapped her wool scarf around her neck.

On Main Street, a heavy-duty pickup with a snowplow attached to the front was clearing one lane, though the snow was persistently covering the just scraped pavement. Hank followed the plow for two blocks and turned left onto the uncleared road that led to Grace's greenhouses at the southeast edge of town. He shifted into low and stayed between 15 and 20 m.p.h. "When we go back, I'll need chains."

Manny and Grace were already moving containers of seedlings on a flatbead carrier that was crunching through the snow. Instead of fluffy powder, it was almost icy.

Seeing Hank and Mikki, they stopped. Grace carefully negotiated the snow. "Thanks for coming. Nice to see you, Mikki. Hank, there's another flatbed in there. Load everything. All of it needs to be kept warm."

"What happened to the heater?"

"Don't know. Plants first, repair second."

The reward for moving the plants was dinner at Grace's. She warmed up a freezer container of beef stew and sliced a loaf of crusty bread. "Best I can do tonight. Do you want beer?"

"Yes."

"Mikki?"

"Maybe not. It'll put me back to sleep."

Hank took the chair opposite Mikki. "I can attest to the sleeping. She slept between Echo and Evergreen."

While Mikki helped Grace clean up, Hank did battle with the chains.

He was still wrestling with the fasteners on the last tire as Mikki left the house. When the fasteners wouldn't lock, there was no swearing. Noah, who was never patient with manual tasks, would have run through his considerable collection of colorful words. Hank was, by comparison, laid back. When he was lecturing her about her hand, especially after Chicago, she would not have guessed he was easy-going. Hank the single father who made grocery lists and helped his mother when asked. But his relationship with his ex probably wasn't so laid back.

"Finally." He stood up, brushing snow off his pants. Seeing Mikki watching him, "You can get in; I'm just going to wash my hands." He returned, carrying a plastic bag, which he carefully stowed on the floor behind his seat. "Breakfast supplies. My mother knows that cold cereal is the only thing on the menu at my place. She's sent bacon and eggs so I can impress you with my culinary skills."

"You know how to cook bacon and eggs?"

"Not as well as my mother."

"I stop at scrambled, and I either overcook or undercook bacon."

"Do you prefer it crispy or greasy?"

"Crispy."

On the drive back to his house, Mikki found herself wondering what else there would be—besides crispy bacon. She was fairly sure he was interested in her. A man did not drive from Houston to New Orleans unless there was "something" on his mind. He'd also willingly picked her up in Greeley, then invited her to go skiing. Yet he hadn't touched her today or said anything to suggest there might be a next stage.

Did she want another stage? In the last few years, she'd pretty much avoided going down that road. A relationship—short or long—hadn't been in her playbook. In truth, Noah—nine years ago—had been her most serious affair. All others came with a sell-by date. Hank, however, was different from most of the men she'd dated or slept with.

Yes, she was ready for the next stage.

The snow chains did their job, but the trip back to Hank's was slow going and, once in the house, she again kept her coat on until the house warmed.

They settled in the living room at each end of the couch, small glasses of white wine within reach on the coffee table. Hank moved a box of watercolor paints and several pages of bright pink flowers onto the floor. "Erin is nagging about having art lessons. She has found some sort of art workshop in July in Estes Park. Is Holly into art?"

Mikki shrugged. "Not that I know of. She's usually trying to read every book she can lay her hands on. She has always been clear that there would be no music lessons of any kind. My family has poisoned that well."

"Did you want piano lessons?"

"Yes, but the classical pieces my mother and other teachers deemed appropriate did not make me love lessons."

"You needed something more upbeat."

She nodded. "My mother never forgot that I went over to the *dark side*—her words. What kind of lessons did you want?"

"Definitely not piano. Guy stuff. Skiing and snowboarding, took a few golf lessons in college—short term lessons."

"Nothing artsy."

He rolled his eyes. "I can't sing or read music, can't draw anything other than stick figures. No instruments. My family's favorite vacation was backpacking. That's it."

"Your mother backpacks?"

"Not any more."

"That's hard."

"Isn't performing hard work?"

She caught her breath. Dangerous territory. "It never felt like it."

"Do what you love and you'll never work a day?"

"I guess." She did not want to talk about performing but, before she could change the subject, he reached across the couch for her left hand, gently turning it over, rubbing his thumb on her palm. "Is it still tight?"

"Not unless I use it a lot. I haven't been playing much since I left New Orleans."

"Do you practice?"

"Always. But the only other time I play is when I'm working on my own compositions."

He was puzzled. "You write music?"

She nodded.

"Is this something new?"

"Not exactly." She was acutely aware that he was still holding her hand—not the examination type of holding. The pressure of his thumb rotating against her palm made it hard to maintain her train of thought. "At Northwestern, jazz piano was my focus, but composing was my minor." She took a deep breath. "When we were on the last tour, Jay began tutoring me, giving me feedback. He even played one of my pieces in London. Now I'm using my previous work and some new pieces as an Independent Study to finish my degree."

Hank was careful not to make the mistake he'd made in New Orleans. He stayed silent, encouraged that she hadn't moved her hand.

After a few minutes, "And no, I don't know what a degree will get me, but I need to finish it before some of the units expire. My father was horrified when I dropped out."

"My mother wasn't thrilled when I walked away from my residency. But you can't do twelve-hour shifts and take care of two little kids. That choice was a no-brainer."

"The fact that Jay wanted me to be in his band made dropping out a no-brainer." She still thought it was the best thing that had happened to her.

"And now?"

"A degree might give me something I can't see yet. I'm certainly not having any luck getting hired."

Wanting to comfort her, he hesitantly raised her hand to his lips.

The brush of the kiss sent a shiver of desire over her. She couldn't move—or think, afraid to break the spell his closeness was wrapping around her. Hank released her hand and slid closer, his hands turning her face to meet his kiss. His mouth open against hers, teasing her to open hers, to let his tongue remind her of that day in Georgetown, willing her to match his passion.

Time stretched as he gently pulled her to her feet, so they were face to face, "Since Georgetown, I've been wanting to kiss you again."

Instead of replying, she leaned into him, lightly kissed his neck, then stayed in the crook of his arm.

In his bedroom, he tugged her sweater over her head, then got stopped by the hooks on her bra.

She pulled back, "Let me."

By the time they fell onto the bed, clothing was strewn across the floor. The explosion of their passion brought them to climax without much foreplay. Later, they took their time, enjoying the journey, exploring, whispering, waiting until they couldn't wait.

Mikki's dreams were usually mismatched swatches of her past. In this dream, she was in Jay's Chicago rehearsal hall—with her mother. Mikki was putting on her ski boots while her mother was doggedly explaining diminished fifth chords. Mikki kept trying to make her mother stop lecturing but was having no luck. Frustrated, she yelled, *Stop*, but no sound came out.

Her heart pounding, she woke with a start, momentarily disoriented, fuzzy around the edges.

The room wasn't familiar, wood paneling, one wall with a sliding glass door that framed fresh snow piled on an otherwise empty patio. The covers on the other side of the bed were thrown back, the pillow squashed into a wrinkled ball that looked totally uncomfortable.

Hank's side.

She closed her eyes. Nudging last night forward, she saw Hank's face. Handsomely sexy, just inches above hers, his eyes narrowing as he brought them to the top of the mountain they'd been climbing.

"Coffee?" As if she'd conjured him, he was standing in the doorway, freshly showered, wearing well-worn Levi's and a dark green Broncos sweatshirt. Holding a coffee mug.

Suddenly shy, Mikki pulled the covers up. "What time is it?"

"Just after ten." As he handed her the mug, he smiled.

"Is the snow still coming down?"

"No, but word is that the schools here will stay closed tomorrow because the buses can't get into some of the outlying areas, so the girls are staying with Taylor another day. Erin is in major sulk mode, which I am gladly letting Taylor deal with."

"No driving to Greeley?"

"Not unless they clear the roads faster than they are right now. I-70 will reopen later; other roads as the plows get to them."

Mikki concentrated on the coffee while she processed the news.

Another day—and night.

With Hank.

Snowed in. Not the worst scenario.

"I'm going to get started on breakfast. I cleaned up the bathroom and found you a new toothbrush. Cate just bought new underwear, so I swiped a pair for you." He smiled as he saw her blush. She wondered how he was going to explain the missing underpants to his teenage daughter.

While letting the shower bring her fully awake, Mikki tried—not successfully—to remind herself that getting in too deep with Hank was not wise. It had been less than a year since the crash. Too soon to give up on performing. As compelling and yes sexy as Hank was, getting entangled could put wider horizons out of reach. In Mikki's experience, there was no such thing as forever.

Hank probably had a sell-by date too.

Before he put the bacon in the skillet, Hank set the rough pine kitchen table for two, even unearthing a package of paper napkins. Not the morning to resort to the usual paper towels he and the girls used.

Last night had been an unexpected gift.

Thank you, weather gods.

Yet caution was warranted. The moment she found a job in the music world, she would be gone. Taylor and Josie revisited. An almost-forty physical therapist with two children versus performing in front of three thousand people. No contest.

Music would win.

While she dried her hair, Mikki turned her phone on and found two texts. One from her father: **Is everything okay at the house?** and one from her sister: **Went to the grocery store early. Saw your car at Hank Duncan's.**

Busted.

She answered her father with **All good**—a hopeful white lie. She didn't answer her sister. Hard to lie about her car being parked in Hank's driveway. But why should she need to? She and Hank were consenting adults who had known one another since June. It might only be a one (or two) night stand, but it wasn't like they'd just met and promptly jumped into bed. She erased both messages.

They lingered over breakfast, adjusting to starting their day together. No longer therapist and patient or acquaintances becoming something else. Having sex—very good sex— changed things.

Mikki cleaned up the kitchen while he went into the living room to phone the clinic.

She was wiping out the sink when he quietly came up behind her, pulled her hair aside, and lightly kissed the back of her neck. She stood very still, her senses spinning. He gently turned her so he could kiss her thoroughly, stopping only when they were both short of breath. "I need to go to the clinic to change tomorrow morning's appointments so I can pick up the girls. Want to keep me company?"

They walked to the clinic, meeting only a woman walking a dog. Mikki was reading an old *National Geographic* in the clinic's lobby when Betty came in, clearly surprised to see Mikki. "Is Hank in his office?"

"Yes. Don't you have today off?"

"I might as well take care of the phone messages; better than being stuck in my apartment." She was scrolling through the voicemail messages on the landline, "Otherwise, tomorrow will be chaos."

Mikki returned to the magazine but was no longer reading. Having others know that she and Hank were—together—was awkward.

On the walk back to his house, they stopped at a small grocery store to buy enough supplies to last until tomorrow. The young girl at checkout was the older sister of one of Cate's friends. Her knowing smile as she handed the plastic bags to Hank told him Cate was going to find out about her father's weekend before he could get ahead of the curve.

After he checked in with Grace and Taylor, reaffirming that he'd pick the girls up by mid-morning, he and Mikki had a late lunch, followed by a replay of last night. An even later dinner, followed by—

A delicious weekend in so many ways.

Once Mikki was back in Greeley, Hank called every night after the girls were asleep. Though she spent her days diligently working on her music, she was also waiting for his call. Suddenly the best part of her day. His voice brought the weekend back, catching at her breath, making her remember his hands on her, the slow smile that hinted he knew everything she was thinking and feeling.

He asked what her day had been like, what she was doing just before he called.

She couldn't see him, but she could tell he was listening, really listening to her answers.

During his Thursday evening call, "Cate asked who was with me at the grocery store on Monday."

"Oops."

"The clerk is the older sister of one of Cate's friends. I figured I'd hear about it sometime."

"What did you tell her?"

"The truth. It doesn't pay to lie to your kids because it'll come back to bite you."

"Does she mind?"

"Not sure. Do you mind her knowing?"

"Guess not. I've never been with a guy who had children."

The calls all ended with "Talk to you tomorrow."

A promise that interfered with her sleep.

In the middle of the following week, "Taylor wants me to bring the girls in late afternoon Friday. She has tickets for a country music jamboree or something that night."

Mikki waited, not sure what she should say.

"Are you busy?"

"No."

"I can come by?"

"Of course."

So quickly the pattern was set.

Nightly phone calls when the girls were with him and, when they were at Taylor's, he stayed in Greeley. They took walks, tried different restaurants. More often than not, they stayed in, taking time to learn about each other, nurturing whatever was growing between them.

By the end of March, there was less snow but no hint of spring. On the girls' Spring Break, Taylor took them to Orlando. Cate had initially protested, "That's for kids," but afterwards Taylor confided, "Don't believe it. She had a great time."

Mikki stayed at Hank's that week.

Because Grace was coming for dinner on Wednesday, Mikki made an early run to Safeway on Tuesday. She and Hank had decided on chili and a garden salad because they could make the chili the night before and, essentially, it was foolproof. Grace promised dessert.

Mikki found herself behind Sophia in the Safeway checkout line. As her sister was retrieving her credit card, "Hi Soph."

Sophia turned quickly; her "Hi" was more surprised than friendly, and she continued out the sliding glass doors. When Mikki exited the store, Sophia was standing outside, waiting for her. A sister trap. Mikki stopped beside her. Might as well get this over with.

Rather than stand in the path of other customers, Mikki asked, "Where are you parked?"

Sophia pointed and they pushed their carts across the lot. Mikki helped her sister unload her cart into the trunk of her car, expecting interrogation but nothing came. Sophia looked haggard, her eyes shadowed underneath.

"Soph, what's wrong?"

Sophia raised her chin slightly, "Don't be nice to me. I'll fall apart."

"Okay, mean it is. You look terrible."

"I know." In a wobbly voice, "Dante and I are in a bad place. I'm scared."

The news wasn't surprising.

"Where's Holly today?"

"Soccer practice. The coach finally got the snow off the field." Sophia pulled her car keys from her pocket. "I can fix lunch or do you have to be somewhere?"

Mikki looked at her basket. "Some of this needs to be in the refrigerator. How about I come by after I put these away. Maybe just a sandwich." Hopefully not a salad.

"Okay."

Mikki had been dreading getting the third degree from her sister. Instead, she might be asking questions about Dante.

While she was unloading the groceries at Hank's, she called his cell and left a voicemail message. "I'm at Sophia's." He always turned his phone off when he had a patient. Amazing how quickly she'd come to know some of his habits. His house was neat, not poison neat. No clothes lying around, no wet towels on the bathroom floor. He was probably better at keeping house than she was. He soaked pans overnight, set up the coffeemaker so it only needed to be switched on in the morning. Mikki's cooking was mostly semi-homemade or take out. Cleaning up was more a matter of throwing out containers. Hank wasn't as neat about paper work, however. Bits of mail and bills didn't seem to have one place to be. Mikki on the other hand had long ago purchased a locking leather brief case that held all her important papers and bills. It served as her file cabinet since she seldom had a permanent home. This was the first time she'd shared personal pieces of her day-to-day life with a lover.

Mikki tiptoed through a ham-and-cheese sandwich lunch, careful not to activate any emotional land mines. She reminded herself to let Sophia choose the conversation. Holly was of course a safe topic. "She was jealous when she found out Erin was going to Orlando."

"Hank says Holly and Erin are really close." Easy way to bring Hank into the conversation.

"I'm glad she has a friend right now."

Mikki waited and when Sophia didn't continue, "Do you want to talk about Dante?"

Sophia shook her head. "Do you want to tell me what's going on with you and Hank?"

"I doubt I have to tell you."

"True. Are you serious or just having fun?"

"Too early to tell. I haven't been in a serious relationship in a long time, well maybe never, so I can't answer the question."

"What will you do if he wants more than fun?"

Mikki shrugged. "No idea. Right now it's a lovely interlude in an otherwise shitty year. Is this temporary with Dante?"

Echoing Mikki. "No idea."

And both fact-finding agendas fizzled. Instead, Sophia talked about her new role with the symphony, and Mikki explained what she was doing with her compositions.

At least they weren't fighting.

Noah's text silently dropped into Mikki's phone just before she woke on Wednesday: **Band booked at Red Rocks over Memorial Day weekend. Wanna play? Call me ASAP.**

Her hands were shaking as she looked for Noah's phone number in her contact list. As soon as he answered, "OMG. Yes."

By the time they broke the connection, her mind was racing, processing the information: Dates, rehearsal times, the phone number of the band's business office, the name of the hotel the band would be booked into. Noah promised to email copies of the music that afternoon. The band was going to hire her. She wanted to shout for joy! No time for an audition, trusting Noah's recommendation. Maybe they'd listened to her solos on the last album.

Two days ago, the band's pianist broke his leg water skiing. He'd had surgery and needed rehab. How long he would be sidelined was unknown. Mikki pulled up several of the band's *You Tube* posts, listening to them over and over. The opportunity to perform made her feel like herself.

Welcome back, Mikki Richards.

She needed to tell someone before she told Hank about Red Rocks—and the possibility there would be other performances while the regular pianist healed.

So she called Teri.

"Mikki, where are you? How are you?"

"At my father's in Greeley and right now very good. What about you?"

"Actually back in Chicago. Glad I kept my condo."

"Working?"

"Doing PR for Concord. Still learning the job. What's up?"

"Have you heard of *Tangerine Slices*?"

"Isn't that the group Noah's with?"

"Yes. Their pianist is sidelined for a while, so they're desperate enough to let me join them. They're scheduled at Red Rocks over Memorial Day weekend. I can hardly believe my luck."

"How's your hand?"

"Mostly okay. But, let's face it, performing is different from practicing. And I now have a lot of new music to learn."

"How can I help?"

"You just did. I needed to run this by someone before I tell—"

"Ah—the physical therapist. It got serious."

"Sort of."

"How long?"

"Two months or so." *Moving into her life a little at a time. Changing it in unexpected ways.* "One thing led to another."

"Are you living together?"

"Not exactly. We spend every other weekend together when his children are with his ex. He's either here or I'm at his place in Evergreen."

"A good guy?"

"Yes." *No argument about that.*

"Love?" As usual, Teri cutting to the chase.

Mikki hadn't yet put her feelings for him into words, into those words. "Could be."

"But he's not about to go on tour as your groupie?"

"Not a chance. He's already been burned by a wife who wanted to wheel and deal on Wall Street more than she wanted to stay with her family. Then there was the girlfriend who went to Ireland for a job and stayed." And now Mikki, who hadn't thought twice about saying yes to Red Rocks and maybe more. She wanted there to be more.

Teri sighed, "Given my track record with men, I'm not the best person to give you relationship advice."

"No worry. Thanks for listening."

Noah sent the music mid-afternoon. Pages and pages. By the time the last sheet slid out, the printer was almost out of ink. Dinner was take out—chicken chow mein. Around ten o'clock, she ate a bowl of ice cream and, at midnight, realized her hand was tightening up, so she went to bed.

In the morning, it had loosened. No swelling. Mikki took that as a good omen and spent the next two days exploring the new music.

When Hank arrived on Saturday morning, he brought warm, chocolate-filled croissants from the bakery near Taylor's condo. The girls always begged him to stop on their way back to Evergreen.

He took his time kissing her. "I've missed you. Is there coffee to go with these?"

"Not yet." She was grateful to have something to keep her hands busy. She was tired after hours of practicing, as well as not getting enough sleep, afraid of what would happen when she told him about Red Rocks. She was probably going to destroy the most loving relationship of her life to jumpstart her career.

Over their second cup of coffee, "Taylor's moving back to New York."

It was hard to tell how he felt, necessitating Mikki's follow up question. "Is that good or bad?"

"Both."

"Do the girls know?"

"She's telling them today. The drive home tomorrow will not be fun."

A Saturday of difficult discussions.

"You didn't want to be there."

"Dealing with Taylor at a distance is better for my blood pressure. But no more Denver weekends for the girls, more important, no more side-trips to Greeley."

About that. Mikki hadn't gotten around to telling him that Greeley would be over anyway when Jon and Ardith returned sometime in July. She really needed a place of her own.

She left space, then, "I have a gig—a temporary job, playing."

"Where?"

"The first one is at Red Rocks in two weeks." Before she lost her nerve, she filled in the details, watching his expression, which unfortunately wasn't giving anything away.

Hank was finding it hard to keep it all sorted. As she rattled off dates, times, and the number of new pieces she needed to learn in the next two weeks, he searched for the right response. He'd never seen her so radiant. An inner switch had been turned on. This was Mikki before the crash. Nothing held back—excited as a child on Christmas morning. He needed to be—should be—happy for her. One piece of his heart was. But the other piece was the one saying *Told ya, one job offer and she's off to grander things.* The Hank Duncan interlude was just that, an interlude. Damn and double damn.

Trapped in his own thoughts, he didn't realize she'd stopped talking and was looking at him expectantly. "What do you think?"

Carefully, "It sounds like a great opportunity. How many other performances?"

"Not sure, maybe four or five. I know one is in Santa Fe. But everything depends on Rick Sollano's leg. It's his right leg so the pedals are an issue. You'll come won't you? to Red Rocks. I can get tickets for you and your family. Not sure about Sophia's schedule, but Holly will love being there."

"Of course I'll be there." Before he said anything that might ruin the mood, he reached across the table for her left hand, massaging it gently. "You've been playing a lot."

"Sort of necessary. The band will arrive a week from Monday so I can rehearse with them. Those'll be long days. I'm nervous. Every group has a different dynamic. They may not like what I do with their music." She retrieved her hand.

In the time it had taken her to tell him about *Tangerine Slices*—where did they get those names?—she'd slipped away from him. Nothing specific or intentional, but she'd moved into a parallel universe he couldn't access. There would be no more leisurely walks, no dinners at new restaurants. No whispered conversations after sex.

The alone-ness he'd been living with before she walked into the clinic would return.

"So should you be working now?"

A tiny nod.

He took the hint. "Okay. I need to get some stuff at Home Depot." He looked at his watch, "Why don't I leave you to it. I'll get lunch somewhere. What time should I come back?"

"Maybe three-ish."

"Done." Wrong word, too close to true.

He leaned across the table, kissed her, and grabbed his jacket. "See you later." He wished they'd gotten to the stage of using the word love. It would have suited him to tell her he loved her instead of a generic "See you later."

Mikki stayed at the table for several minutes, trying to decide whether he was upset and unwilling to admit it or whether he was being supportive—an overused phrase—providing space and time for her to work.

No matter, she still had three pieces she hadn't touched. She poured herself more coffee and put the music for the first piece on the rack.

As it had always been, when she was immersed in taking a new piece apart, she lost track of time and missed meals. Not until she heard the front door open—and glanced at her watch, did she realize she was ravenous and needed to pee. She passed him on the way to the bathroom—"Hi." When she came back, she stopped in front of him and kissed him. "Sorry, emergency. I'm starving. I think I missed lunch. Can we go for an early dinner?"

Hank didn't go to Home Depot. He walked around downtown aimlessly, thinking of nothing and everything, and finally stopped at a Burger King, lingering over coffee he did not need, trying to unscramble his reaction to Mikki's news. And secondarily, Taylor's return to New York. The girls, well Cate, would be upset. Two upsets at once. He hated drama.

This would be his last weekend in Greeley. Two weeks from tomorrow was the performance. Two weeks afterward, Taylor was returning to New York. He'd be back to having the girls full time and working.

It hadn't been a problem before, but it felt like it was going to be a problem now.

He was standing still while the women in his life went here and there, entering his life, then leaving him where he'd been in the first place. Once upon a time, he'd imagined living a surgeon's life: repairing lives, his family there for him, enough money to explore the world beyond the operating room. Yet here he was on the fringes of the medical world, earning enough but, as the girls got older, grateful for Taylor's support checks. He was leading the life that women complained about, tied down with children, not fulfilling their dreams. Irony in there somewhere.

Mikki's arrival on his office doorstep nearly a year ago was a gift. As the months passed, he'd been telling himself he wasn't second-guessing the outcome of their relationship, but he wanted more time. Not necessarily marriage, but more time.

That evening, they drove into Denver to a Thai restaurant they'd heard about. No discussion about Red Rocks or New York, neither wanting to damage the weekend any further.

Mikki awoke early Sunday—her mind racing, the new music bouncing around in her head. Then there was the logistics of moving to the hotel near Red Rocks, what she would wear for the performance. She needed a haircut. She turned to look at Hank, deeply asleep, his dark hair tumbling over his forehead. He slept neatly, no snoring, mouth closed.

If she moved or touched him, he'd wake with half a smile and breakfast would be delayed. His morning disposition was typically better than hers. Often, she was slow to come alive. She gently touched his cheek and waited for the smile.

He usually picked the girls up in Denver at three. An hour's drive home, dinner, last minute homework, everyone early to bed. Sometimes he called Mikki before he fell asleep.

But today Taylor called just before one. "You need to come now." Taylor specialized in declarative sentences.

"What's wrong?"

Mikki stopped sorting the pages of music.

Suddenly impatient. "Okay, okay, it'll be an hour." He ended the call. "What?"

"Cate is pitching a fit because she wants to go to New York with Taylor, finish high school there. Taylor has never figured out how to manage the girls. When they don't do what she wants them to do, she panics, loses patience, and then loses the war." He checked his watch. "Come sit with me."

She set the music aside and curled up against him on the couch, her head on his shoulder. He kissed the top of her head. "Please don't go back to blonde. I like you as a brunette."

"Umm, I was actually thinking of red this time; brown is boring." She waited.

"Seriously?"

She laughed. "No, just messing with you. I've gotten used to having it natural."

After a few minutes, he asked the question he knew the answer to. "You're really happy about Red Rocks?"

"Oh God, yes. It's who I am."

He wasn't brave enough to argue the point. He hadn't known her long enough to have evidence to back up his belief that there was, could be, so much more in her life. Work wasn't everything. She'd seldom left the bubble of performing long enough to find out if there were other parts to her. Other things she might want. Like love. Not just sex, but something more complete. Her experiences in the real world were narrow, even narrower than his. Sometimes he wondered if he'd lived too narrow a life, taken the easy road when it came to revamping his professional goals. But children shouldn't have to raise themselves. And at the same time, children couldn't be everything in a life. He'd tried to maintain balance. Until Mikki had tipped his settled life. Made him feel things he'd set aside while he was raising the girls. Sexy without trying. Funny. She didn't mind his teasing or his bullying about using her hand. They were easy with each other—that was evident even in New Orleans. She was strong, yes, not willing to live a life that someone or something else dictated. There was still a thread of anger about her hand, about losing a life that was everything to her.

She was five years younger. The things a person learned and did when they were in their twenties hadn't fit into her performing, on-the-road life. She hadn't struggled for money until the demise of the band. Lived in hotels and on buses instead of having roommates. What did a single father with limited financial prospects and no knowledge of music have to offer?

Sadness followed him from Greeley into Denver, where female hysteria met him head on. Cate was, as always, at the center of the chaos.

"Why can't I move to New York? It's not fair." Her go-to line when she feared she was losing an argument. Hank sat next to her. Across the room, Taylor was pacing nervously. Erin was nowhere to be seen. Probably hiding in her bedroom. She did not do conflict well.

Taylor stopped pacing. "I told her I keep long hours. Sometimes I work all weekend. She's too young to be on her own, even though my building has top of the line security. New York is not safe."

Cate glared at her mother. "Yet you live there."

"Yes."

Cate tried again, "It's an excellent school, you said so yourself. I'd be better prepared for college than I will be if I stay in Evergreen."

Hank let Cate and Taylor revisit the dispute, calculating his next move. He didn't want Cate in New York for Taylor's reasons and his own. He'd miss her; there was so little time left before graduation. And Taylor might not be the best influence on a full time basis.

He waded in.

"Your mother and I agreed long ago that living in Evergreen was better for you girls. That hasn't changed. You are not going to New York. Gather up your stuff. We need to get on the road."

After Cate's bedroom door slammed, Taylor sighed, "That went well. Can you handle this? She's going to be hell on wheels for a while."

Hank rubbed his hand over his hair. "Yes she will." Taylor's actions always left a mess he had to clean up. He hoped Grace wasn't too busy this week. He might need rescuing.

"Erin tells me there's a new woman in your life. Serious?"

Ah, the Holly/Erin pipeline.

"Yes there is. But it's early days. She's a musician. Not given to small town domesticity. Are they ready to leave?"

Taylor stood up. "Let me get them moving."

Jay Mercury had always been afraid of over confidence, afraid the band members might rest on their laurels and not perform at their highest levels. He was quick to remind them they were only as good as their next performance, encouraging them to be at the top of their game every time.

Tough love.

Tonight Mikki had to be at the top of her game: for Jay, for this new band, and to prove to herself her hand was healthy. A make or break moment. In the days leading up to the performance, Hank called in the evening, letting her de-program her day. She was nervous and excited all at once, though he could tell by her voice that she was tired. It was all he could do not to ask about her hand, not to show up at the hotel in Morrison to do his physical therapist schtick. He described the girls' fifth grade promotion ceremony. Holly had not been understanding when Mikki told her she couldn't attend. "You love music more than you love me."

Rehearsing with four new musicians, plus Noah and vocalist Sienna, was stressful, and not being memorized felt awkward. Watching the music interfered with her being able to improvise. Fortunately, her years with Jay had provided coping skills she'd forgotten she had.

Tangerine Slices was BG's, Bill Gale's, baby. Except for Noah, the band had worked together for three years, just now beginning to get some traction within the jazz scene. They were all helpful, needing her to do her best so they could do theirs. After each rehearsal, Noah stayed behind with Mikki so she could ask questions, get his take on what she was doing and what she should change. Because significant others were banned for the week—she and Noah had dinners together, then spent the evenings in their rooms, resting up.

The day of the performance, Mikki did only what was necessary, taking a short nap in the afternoon, eating a light dinner before getting on the hotel shuttle that took the band to Red Rocks for the last minute sound check.

Red Rocks Amphitheatre never disappointed. The tilted blocks of red sandstone created a natural backdrop for the stadium seating that looked onto the stage and the endless Colorado prairie to the east. Hazy in the daytime—after dark, city lights and stars.

Though the powers that be had, over the years, added a visitor center and shops to the venue, the star of Red Rocks was still the soaring monoliths cradling the stage and audience. *Gaining Ground* had performed there three years ago. That time, none of Mikki's family attended. Jon and Ardith were in Europe, and the symphony had a performance at Boettcher Hall. This time, she got comp tickets for Hank's family and one for Holly because, once again, Sophia had a performance of her own. Grace would bring Holly, and Hank would collect his girls from Taylor's.

At 7:45, the band members began wandering onto the stage one at a time. No grand entrance, casually settling in, then sliding into the music, sneaking up on the audience. At the end of the first selection, applause thundered into the twilight, and Mikki let the magic of adrenalin wrap itself around her.

The music was not what Hank had come for. He only saw Mikki wearing a filmy multi-colored skirt, sandals, and a tank top that left her arms free. Her hair was loose down her back, the sides pulled away from her face into a single braid.

Grace was sitting between Erin and Holly, a tactic designed to minimize giggling and any other disruptive behaviors. Until the floodlights dimmed, Cate occupied herself with her phone, anything to keep from having to talk to her father. He'd been getting the silent and/or minimal-answer treatment for two weeks.

A new family record.

For Mikki, the performance sped by. About two-thirds through, she had a fifteen-minute break while the guitars and horns dominated the stage. She sat on a straightback chair behind the side curtains, sipping water. She couldn't see beyond the lights, but somewhere out there Hank was watching and listening. His being in the audience provided a special dimension. Then she was back at the piano. Immersed in the final pieces, playing two encores.

The applause bounced off the rocks. One by one, BG called the band members to center stage to take a bow, to savor the appreciation. When Mikki took her bow, Hank added a piercing whistle, thumb and index finger against his teeth.

Startled, Grace turned, "You can still do that?"

"Don't have much call to use it. Can you?"

"Not since I got my partial."

Cate looked like she'd like to disappear. "Dad, you're too old to do that."

He grinned. "Who says?"

Hank was relieved the evening had gone well for Mikki—at least it seemed so to him. He was looking forward to—well—many things. Yet, hovering around the edges of his thought was the possibility that she was poised to move beyond his reach, might already be moving. Tonight he'd finally seen the professional Mikki Richards. Remembering the non-professional Mikki, he caught himself wondering whether the disparate pieces of their lives could fit together. They lived in such different worlds.

As the audience was disappearing into the darkness beyond the amphitheater, Hank lagged behind Grace and the children, wanting to find Mikki. Grace was returning Erin and Cate to Taylor's; then she and Holly would drive to Evergreen. Hank would collect his girls tomorrow afternoon as he always did on a three-day weekend.

Hank hoped to spend the night with Mikki, either in Morrison or in Greeley. But they hadn't made plans. Uncertainty caught up with him at the performers' entrance as he waited for her. Their loosely knit relationship—what cynics might call bi-weekly booty calls—might not include the assumption of staying in her hotel room.

The instant joy of seeing her walking toward him alongside Noah, as she was right now, reminded him this was love. Hank let them come to where he was standing. He was tempted to pull her into his arms and kiss her until they were both short of breath. But she stayed next to Noah. She was nervous, "Hank, Noah. Noah, Hank." The men briefly shook hands. Not much else to do, and Hank couldn't think of anything polite to say. This was not the reunion he'd imagined.

Mikki filled the moment, "We're meeting the rest of the band in the hotel bar to unwind. Want to come?"

"Sure." *Not really. I'd rather have you to myself.*

"You know where it is?"

So she was riding with Noah? "Yes."

"We have to catch the shuttle back. It's waiting."

Only slightly better.

He stayed in his car until he saw the band members go into the hotel, watched as a porter unloaded the sound equipment. Then waited another ten minutes, afraid to let his eagerness show. He wanted to hold her; instead he would be an outsider in her world.

It had been hours since Mikki had eaten. Now, sitting between Noah and Hank, she was devouring bar food while drinking a Tecate beer. The noise of the bar making it impossible to have a conversation. Musicians were usually keyed up after a performance, like college students at the end of final exams.

The bar emptied gradually. Noah disappeared a little after midnight, checking a missed call on his cell. Undoubtedly his girlfriend.

Hank needed to ask what he hadn't asked: *Do you want me to stay?*

Circling the question, "Are you exhausted?"

She smiled, "In a good way. The crash will come later."

"How much later?"

"Much later." She leaned against him, "Did you pack a toothbrush?"

"I did." And his evening improved.

They'd barely gotten into her room before they were awkwardly dropping clothing, laughing as they tumbled onto the bed. Hungrier than they'd realized. No foreplay required.

Much later, Mikki rested in the curve of his arm. "I missed you."

"Clearly."

"You missed me too."

"Clearly."

As she'd predicted, the crash arrived. She dropped into a deep sleep, not waking until lines of morning sun edged the window blinds. Hank awoke a little later, his arm numb beneath her.

It was mid-morning by the time they went to the hotel coffee shop in search of breakfast. Hank opted for bacon and pancakes; Mikki ordered scrambled eggs, potatoes and sausage. "I am starving."

He reached across the table for her left hand. He lightly massaged the knuckles. "It doesn't feel tight. Any problems after last night?"

She shook her head. "But if I had another performance tonight, I might notice it. In between rehearsals last week, I kept the brace on."

His cell phone, lying on the table, vibrated. He looked at the screen. To Mikki: "It's Erin." Into the phone: "Hey." Silence. "Three o'clock as usual." Silence, "I'll try." More silence. "Yes. See you later."

"Problems?"

"Just an overly observant child. She asked if I was with you. Hard to fool children."

"Did your mother tell?"

"Doubtful. We try to maintain a united front on all topics." He poured himself more coffee from the carafe on the table. "Now that this performance is over, what's on your agenda?"

"I need to send my Independent Study compositions to the university by July."

"How long will it take to find out if you graduate?"

She shrugged. "Whenever the department gets around to listening to the recordings."

"Are you happy with what you've done?"

"Mostly, but I'm sure I'll need to make changes."

Their food arrived. Mikki swiped a slice of his bacon. "It smells so good."

"No fair."

She laughed. He loved that she knew she could give him trouble.

In the midst of getting the girls organized for the return to Evergreen, Taylor remarked—a little too casually—"Erin says your girlfriend is the pianist in the band that was at Red Rocks last night."

He wasn't sure that *girlfriend* was the right label but, given Erin's age, *lover* would be a bit graphic. "Yes. She's filling in for their regular pianist."

"Is this serious? Erin says it is."

Time to talk to Erin about over-sharing with Taylor.

"Does she now." He didn't want to discuss Mikki with Taylor, not ready to talk to anyone about what was going on.

And Taylor moved into the next difficult discussion. "I've given my notice here for the last week of June."

He waited, feeling there was more, "Cate wants to come to New York with me. Stay until school starts here."

"Will Cate be on her own?" He did not want her wandering New York while Taylor was working.

"All on her own, she found a four week science workshop for high school students at NYU. She'll be there all day. I promise to keep her safe. I'm not really that unreliable."

Probably not the time to take issue. "I'll look at the workshop online and talk to her." So Cate had figured out how to get a little bit of New York since he wouldn't let her move there for the school year. Clever. He needed to remember she was Taylor's daughter. Taylor had always been good at figuring out how to get what she wanted.

The trip to Evergreen was unusually silent. Cate wisely did not bring up going to New York with Taylor. As soon as the girls were in bed, Hank called Grace, his sounding board of choice.

"Maybe you should put a tracker on her phone or is that illegal?"

"Not a bad idea. I'll see what I can find out, though she'd probably never speak to me again. Thanks for taking care of the girls last night."

"Mikki's really talented. I loved the music. I assume you two found one another?"

"Yes." No more details.

"My son of the one word answers."

"Bye Mom." He called Mikki. And afterwards wished he hadn't heard her news.

"I'm going to Santa Fe with the band a week from Saturday. Then to Albuquerque the following weekend." *And then where?*

The thing he'd greatly feared was happening. He wanted to be happy for her, but it was hard to be happy and unhappy at the same time. She didn't seem to notice he wasn't as enthusiastic as she was, rattling off the details of the next few weeks. She had accepted without even mentioning it to him.

After they said goodbye, Hank went in search of the very expensive bottle of scotch he kept for special or disastrous occasions. Tonight qualified as disastrous. Taylor and Cate would be leaving Denver. Mikki would be in Santa Fe, and he and Erin would be in Evergreen.

Mikki was so excited about the additional performances that she quite honestly hadn't factored in Hank. Not until she was telling Sophia about the band's schedule—and Sophia asked how Hank fit into Mikki's return to the stage—did she realize what she hadn't done. And she didn't know how to fix it without jeopardizing the opportunity to play.

Once Mikki was in New Mexico with *Tangerine Slices*, Sophia and Holly moved into Jon and Ardith's house for a few days, explaining to Jon that she needed time to think. Her story to Holly involved shopping and a day at Elitch's, a mid-summer treat in lieu of summer camp. With Dante, however, she didn't pull any punches, letting him know how angry she was about his continuing neglect of the family. He was still sleeping in the workshop once or twice a week. Her parting line—*We may not come back*—was harsher than she'd intended, but she was tired of pretending their life was okay. Surprisingly, being harsh paid off. The Tuesday after they went to Greeley, Dante reluctantly agreed to meet with a counselor. Sophia made an appointment for Friday, not giving him time to change his mind.

Today's Dante was not the Dante she'd known since they dated in high school. Then, he was always laughing. Doing only enough schoolwork to stay on the track team. Handsome. He could have had his pick of girls, but he only had eyes for Sophia.

Dante's paternal grandfather established Perillo Furnishings; his son Luis took over the business when Dante was ten, so furniture, in one way or another, had always been part of his life. After high school, because he wanted to design rather than just sell furniture, he earned an apprenticeship with a noted New England craftsman and was gone for two years.

When he returned to Colorado, Dante established Perillo Woods in a small rented warehouse near Aurora. His father had to co-sign on the lease. By the time he and Sophia married, the business was inching along, sometimes in the black. By that time, Sophia was in the Symphony so there was at least one steady paycheck.

This last year something had shifted. A two-career marriage was pretty much the twenty-first century norm, so why couldn't they make it work? Holly was at an age where she could look after herself in many ways: showers, choosing what to wear and getting dressed, keeping her room neat, doing her homework. The major issue was that Sophia did not want Holly home alone or sitting on the curb outside school, waiting for her father to pick her up.

Holly, of course, told Erin and Erin told Hank that Sophia and Holly were staying at the house in Greeley: "And they went to Elitch's. I love going there." This, on the morning Erin was beginning her summer job at Grace's—a job she'd begged for. "Cate's off doing her New York thing, so can I have her job?" A year of weekends with Taylor had made both girls noticeably more assertive. Probably not a bad thing—still, it took some getting used to.

In the three weeks Mikki had been gone, there had been no phone calls or texts. During their last breakfast at the hotel in Morrison, Mikki read off *Tangerine Slices'* upcoming schedule of performances as he wrote down the dates: Santa Fe, Albuquerque, Dallas, and St. Louis, ending in Chicago. Of course, whenever the band's regular pianist returned, Mikki would again be unemployed and without a place to live. The downside of her nomadic lifestyle.

They kissed goodbye in the hotel parking lot, neither mentioning the future. Hank wanted stability for his girls; Mikki didn't seem to need roots.

And so an awkward, emotional distance filled the geographical distance between them. As the days passed, he was more and more certain their worlds were too different.

In the deepest part of his being, he missed her.

Except for Noah, *Tangerine Slices'* cast of musicians was as different as their music. But on performance nights, as soon as the opening notes swept over the stage, the thrill was the same as it had always been for Mikki. Almost like being with *Gaining Ground*. On the nights they weren't performing, however, boredom set in. The sameness of hotel rooms had never bothered her before; now the hours dragged. To complicate matters, Hank insisted on invading her dreams, reminding her of his steady gentleness, the way they laughed together. He hadn't called and she was unsure whether she should call him. By choosing to go on this tour, she had sent a message: *My career is more important than you are.* And he'd obviously received it. She had no right to expect him to sit around until she had time for him.

How had she ended up with no place of her own except a series of piano benches. No one was paying attention to whether she was happy or tired or scared. Not even Noah. Little by little, she was losing the joy of performing. Music had always been enough. It might not be enough any more.

On a lunch break in St. Louis, hot dogs on a park bench alongside a food truck, Noah told her that he and Caron were getting married. Mikki shouldn't have been surprised by the news because Caron had shown up at each venue. But she was surprised that Noah was committing to one woman. Uncharacteristically conventional. Mikki didn't know Caron all that well. Petite, long jet black hair and, in Mikki's view, too much makeup. But she was good to Noah so Mikki was on board.

"When?"

"August." Then the other shoe dropped. "She's two months pregnant."

And the pieces of the puzzle fell into place.

Noah was exiting Mikki's life. He'd changed in ways she hadn't noticed. She'd been too busy clinging to a life that didn't seem to want her anymore, only getting her foot in the door, temporarily peeking inside. Clearly, she'd overstayed her welcome.

The three Chicago performances played to packed houses, fans enthusiastically dancing in the aisles, asking for encore after encore. *Tangerine Slices* was perhaps at the top of its game like *Gaining Ground* had been. But this time, it wasn't Mikki's game.

Rick showed up at the after-party, using a cane but ready to play again. He would fly back to LA with the band. Mikki was, once again, unemployed with no plans other than turning in her final compositions at Northwestern. Though Teri had attended one of the performances, Mikki didn't have the nerve to ask if she could stay with her.

During her parents' appointment with the marriage counselor—the name on the door was Dr. Steven Lowe—Holly sat in the waiting room, armed with a library book, her phone, and snacks. The first thing she did was text Erin, asking whether she could stay with her at Grace's. She needed to get her father to take her back to Evergreen this afternoon. **I want to go to soccer practice tomorrow and I'm pretty sure my mom's gonna stay here.**

Erin's **Great** came fifteen minutes later. Next step, getting her parents to agree. The days in Greeley hadn't been as much fun as she'd hoped. Her mother was preoccupied, tense, not nearly as patient as she usually was. Holly needed time with Erin and her soccer teammates. Adult unhappiness was wearing.

The counseling appointment lasted almost an hour. When the office door finally opened, her mother looked as though she'd been crying and her father's mouth was clamped tight, as though he might cry too. No smile for Holly.

Surprisingly, they didn't argue when Holly suggested Burger King for lunch, but the silence between her parents was deafening. Halfway through their meal, she made her pitch. "Dad, can I go back with you and stay over with Erin? I need to go to soccer practice tomorrow. I can't get behind."

Before Dante answered, Sophia intervened, "I thought she was working at the greenhouse, staying with Grace."

"She is. There's a double bed."

Sophia scrolled to Grace's phone number and touched the screen.

Holly finished her hamburger, listening to her mother's side of the conversation, getting the sense that she would be going to Evergreen.

Sophia put her phone away and, for the first time since they entered the restaurant, looked directly at Dante. "Do you mind delivering her to Grace Duncan's today? I have a rehearsal tonight."

Dante nodded. "Okay."

Holly breathed a sigh of relief.

Sophia hadn't expected much from the counseling appointment. Talking about emotional/personal problems had never been easy for Dante. Because his family had always been shouters, Dante generally retreated in the face of any kind of conflict.

Sophia had texted Ardith, still in New Hampshire, asking her to recommend a counselor: "Please don't tell my dad." The high school kept a list of professional therapists and psychiatrists in case parents wanted to seek professional help for their children. Instead of texting her answer, Ardith called: "I've never met Dr. Lowe, but I hear good things. He handles all issues relating to families."

His office was unpretentious, which fit his low-key demeanor perfectly. Probably late forties, his already graying hair receding. Slacks and a short sleeve cotton shirt. His receptionist had a small cubicle separate from the waiting room, giving patients privacy.

The first thing Sophia noticed was his easy smile, how quietly he spoke, letting Dante start the session by answering a broad, direct question: "How do you feel about your relationship with your daughter?"

For months, Sophia had been assembling lists of Dante's flaws, the times when he forgot to pick Holly up or missed her soccer games, self-righteously ignoring whatever part she may have played in what was rapidly destroying their family. She'd come ready to accuse him. Get Dr. Lowe on her side. But Dante had the floor and was sincerely and articulately answering the question, finishing with "I love my daughter. I don't spend enough time with her."

Dr. Lowe's second question was "How do you feel about your wife?"

Dante ended his answer with "I've loved her since I was sixteen."

Without permission, tears slipped down Sophia's cheeks.

"And last, tell me about your business."

Dante didn't answer right away. He looked down, then softly, "It's failing. I'm failing."

Sophia couldn't believe what she was hearing, "But you're always busy and you've added employees."

Startled by her interruption, "Not failing financially. But there's less and less creativity. I'm failing at what I set out to do. We're busy because I need to pay my employees, keep them busy. As a result, I'm not creating. I'm doing *business*—he spat out the word. "I'm failing myself." He looked straight at Sophia: "What if you could only play nursery rhymes instead of the classical pieces you love?"

Sophia couldn't think of what to say. Wasn't sure she could be as honest as he'd just been. So ashamed of the mental lists she'd been keeping.

Dr. Lowe turned to Sophia. "Do you want to say something?"

"I didn't know," and she began to cry.

Summer thunderstorms are expected in the high country. They arrive, seemingly from nowhere, crackling and crashing over the front range until they grumble off to the east and fall apart over the prairie. But when a small storm joins forces with a larger weather front, the noise and rain increase and lightning becomes more dangerous. Early Sunday morning, a lightning storm blew over Mt. Evans and quickly kindled a blaze that, since it was dark and in a remote area, no one noticed until dawn. By then, it already had a running start.

Because Grace kept a small TV set on in the greenhouse while she was working, she heard about the fire around 10 a.m. She'd left cold cereal and fruit out for the girls' breakfast. Erin had promised to work two hours sometime today; Sophia had texted that she'd pick Holly up mid-afternoon. Grace called Hank's cell. "Where are you?"

"At the Clinic. I'm way behind on paperwork. Why?"

"There's a fire between Evergreen and Mt. Evans." She repeated what she'd heard. "Do you have a TV over there?"

"No, but we still have the police scanner. I'll listen in. How are the girls?"

"Hopefully, fixing their breakfasts. They were up way too late, giggling."

Dante spent the morning sanding a dining room table and, only when he left the workshop to see what was in the fridge for lunch, did he see black smoke billowing to the southwest. Much too close. The light blinking on the landline in the kitchen was a robo announcement of immediate evacuations south of Evergreen.

Having listened to the frantic chatter on the scanner, a worried Hank was at Grace's when she received the same robo call, listing the locations of evacuation centers and where to take large animals. Because Grace refused to leave until she had the greenhouse sprinklers set and loaded her business computer and important files in the van, Hank drove the girls to an elementary school just off I-70, then returned to the Clinic. Grace and Manny evacuated an hour later, each driving a Duncan Gardens van. Grace went to the evac center; Manny went home to Kittridge, where Tina was anxiously watching the fire coverage.

Dante called Sophia to warn her off: "You should stay where you are. Holly and Erin are at Country Day evacuation center with Grace. The roads are going to be jammed and some of the secondary roads are already closed."

"Where are you?"

"At our place, I'm hosing down the house but, by the looks of this thing, a garden hose won't help much."

"Please leave. You don't want to get trapped."

"I don't want to lose the house."

As scared as Sophia was, it occurred to her that he'd said *house*—not workshop.

Mikki was on standby in O'Hare, hoping for a seat on the 10:40 a.m. flight to Denver. The airport was crammed with summer travelers, barely an empty seat in the Delta area. Though there were several TV monitors, she wasn't paying attention to the Breaking News about a massive wildfire near Denver because she was reading the reviews of *Tangerine Slices'* Chicago performances on her phone. Most of them complimentary.

Two and a half hours later, as the plane approached DIA, thick smoke was hiding the mountains, blocking the sun. More black smoke than white. Never a good sign.

While she waited for her luggage, she called Sophia.

"Are you still at Dad's? Where's the fire? I could see smoke as we landed."

"You're in Denver?" Once again Mikki had failed to warn anyone she was coming back. Unless Hank knew.

"Yes. I'm waiting for my suitcase. I'll catch the shuttle." Asking Sophia to pick her up would undoubtedly not go down well.

"The fire's close to our place and probably Grace's. The girls are at Country Day. It's an evacuation center. Hank dropped them off a few hours ago and, by now, Grace should be with them. Dante's still at our place, using a garden hose, trying to save our house. I'm leaving in a few minutes to check on the girls, take clean clothes for Holly. They may be at the school for a while. I'm hoping Dante evacuates too."

"What can I do?"

Sophia almost said *Nothing, like usual*, then went with "I need to go," and she broke the connection.

Mikki saw her suitcase approaching, grabbed it, and followed the signs to Ground Transportation.

Thank God for the house in Greeley, but the family B n B was about to go back to its owners. She should look at apartment rentals online. She needed a place. Needed to get her furniture out of storage. Make a life of some kind since no one seemed ready to make one for her.

By the time the shuttle dropped her off at Ardith's, the sky was dark with drifting smoke. Once she showered, Mikki settled in front of the TV with a bowl of cold cereal and milk that was close to going bad.

The Evans fire coverage was on every channel. The flames were being pushed by strong westerly winds, forcing evacuations on the south end of Evergreen and several smaller communities to the west and south. Colorado Wildfire was cautioning everyone to stay out of the area. Stronger winds were forecast overnight. Hot-shot crews from Montana were being brought in because the strength of the winds would make fighting the fire from the air impossible until the next day.

Mikki listened to evacuees being interviewed, watched video clips of the scorched topography. Scary images. She wondered how close the fire was to Sophia's and to Evergreen itself. What if the town was destroyed? What about Hank's house and the Clinic? When Mikki left Greeley after high school, she'd been sure she didn't have any emotional connection to the area. Her mother's death and, a few years later, Jon moving in with Ardith fueled her *I don't belong there anymore* attitude. But being temporarily in Evergreen last year had reconnected her to Colorado.

Suddenly, she was afraid.

She called Sophia's cell. "Are you okay? Where are you?"

"I'm with the girls and Grace at the evac center." Her voice wobbled, "It doesn't look good for Evergreen. And Dante's not answering his phone."

Mikki switched off the TV. "I'll be there as soon as I can. Is I-70 open?"

"I think so. Get off at Highway 74 Exit. There are police everywhere, directing the evacuation." Sophia almost sounded glad Mikki was coming.

At the same time Sophia and Mikki were talking, Erin called her father.

"Hey sweetheart. Everything okay?"

"Sort of. Gran's here. But Holly is really worried about her dad. He's not answering his phone. Could you maybe check on him?"

"I don't know if I can drive into that area. They're getting ready to evacuate the whole town."

"Will our house burn down?"

"Hope not."

"Where would we live?" Always Erin's first worry. He could tell she was close to crying. He needed to be with her. But first he needed to track down Holly's dad. He locked up the Clinic and drove toward Perillo Woods.

When Mikki got close to the Highway 74 exit, there were signs directing fire evacuees to the sprawling charter school. The parking lot was full, vehicles spilling onto an adjacent grassy field. Smoke was hanging everywhere.

At the entrance to the gym, she gave her name and Sophia's address to the teenage girl sitting at a table. "I'm visiting my sister." She found the girls, Sophia, and Grace in a far corner sitting on cots; the girls were staring at their phones.

Holly slid over so Mikki could sit beside her. Mikki kissed the top of her niece's head. "Hi Hol."

A mumbled "Hi."

"Scared?"

Holly nodded.

"Me too." She pulled Holly into the circle of her arm and half-smiled at Sophia, who looked terrified. "Any news?"

Sophia shook her head. "Erin said Hank's going out to our place to try to find him."

Mikki's stomach flipped over. She'd assumed Hank would be at the Clinic, in the middle of town. Safe.

Grace stood up abruptly. "The Red Cross is setting up food tables. I'll see if I can help. I have to do something." In faded jeans and the clogs she wore in the greenhouses, she made her way outside, taller than most of the women who were putting out sandwiches and bottles of water. Oddly enough, Grace's presence was reassuring.

Dante had waited too long.

The heat and smoke were making him lightheaded. The gravel road perpendicular to his driveway was blocked by flames licking at the ground cover, sending orange fingers up the trunks of the Lodgepole pines that circled the property. He calculated the odds of driving the truck through the blaze across the driveway. If he gunned the truck, kept the windows rolled up against the smoke, he might have a chance. If he stood where he was much longer, he would be incinerated. In the few seconds he was debating what to do, a flaming branch dropped onto the workshop roof. A tinderbox of dry wood and chemicals. Ten years of his heart and soul. The metal siding would be no match for the wind and fire destroying everything he'd worked for. He pulled his keys from his pocket and started the truck, backed up, then floor boarded through the flames, hoping for an opening beyond.

Hank knew most of the roads and tracks that crisscrossed the land south of Evergreen. When his mother was looking for land to build the greenhouses, they had covered every inch. But today, because the smoke reduced visibility to about a car length, he was losing the sense of where he was. Shoulders tense, he was gripping the steering wheel so tightly his hands hurt. The drone of a plane filled the air, low, probably preparing to drop retardant. Once it was dark, the planes would be grounded.

The Perillo property was half a mile, as the crow flies, from Grace's greenhouses, but the only road that connected the properties was two miles of crumbling asphalt winding through the trees. Hank's three-year old SUV wasn't built for off-road adventures, but there wasn't any other choice. Flames were directly ahead and along the right side, tendrils of smoke around the base of the trees, occasional hot spots reigniting. Hank was cursing himself for putting himself at risk just because Dante Perillo didn't have the sense to follow evacuation orders. Hank had the girls to think of. The SUV bumped this way and that, telling him he needed to slow down.

As soon as he left the fence line he'd been following, he saw the silver, heavy-duty pick up crushed against a blackened tree. Perillo Woods was lettered on the driver's door. At the same moment, Hank realized he'd pulled over too far into the soft edge. There was no traction, his wheels spinning. He got out and jogged to the truck, pulling the driver's door open. Unconscious, Dante was trapped by the steering wheel which was pushing him against the seat, blood running from a gash on his forehead. Instinctively, Hank laid his fingers on Dante's neck underneath the jawbone, feeling for a pulse. Still alive. Hank's mind went into overdrive, looking for solutions. Prying him out of the truck was imperative, but moving him also came with dangers. The steering wheel was jammed against his torso. His left arm was dangling.

Hank pulled his cell phone from his back pocket, hoping the satellite was working in spite of the smoke. He had only half a bar.

No connection. He walked away from the truck, back toward the road. Suddenly he had one bar. He hit the emergency service number in his phone. No answer. "Come on, come on; pick up."

After five minutes, a voice, barely audible, "What's your emergency?"

Hank explained who he was and where he was, about Dante's condition, the closeness of the fire. The voice on the other end remained calm in spite of Hank's voice rising. Yelling would not make the help come any faster—or at all. Then the connection disappeared.

Maybe a text instead. He tapped Grace's number. Typed in **Mom, SOS. Stone cairn. Dante's seriously hurt. Need help.** He hit send and hoped the message actually went somewhere.

He might as well assume help wasn't coming and get on with whatever he could figure out on his own.

If Dante had a serious head wound, moving him could further damage what was already damaged, but leaving him in a truck filled with gasoline in the midst of a wildfire was even more dangerous. He looked into the bed of the pickup and saw a pile of canvas tarps. One of those might just help him get Dante to a safe spot.

It took Hank ten minutes to lower Dante to the ground. He used his pocket knife to cut the padding away from the back of the driver's seat, giving him extra inches to move Dante, a little at a time, away from the steering wheel, through the open door, finally easing him down onto the tarp spread out on the ground and pulling the tarp away from the truck. Moving dead weight was harder than he'd thought. He'd gotten soft. If he lived through this, he needed to spend some time at a gym. The exertion, intense heat and dense smoke made him feel as though he were going to pass out. Before he fell down, he sat down. Then lay down on the bare ground beside the tarp, turned onto his stomach and pulled his arms up so his face rested on them, with a small air pocket beneath his face.

Before he drifted off, he wondered where Mikki was.

The Red Cross sandwiches disappeared fast—bologna and cheese, a little mayo. Anything tasted good when you hadn't eaten all day and were scared. Mikki couldn't remember if she'd ever before tasted bologna. Her mother hadn't considered it nutritious.

Once the tables were cleared, more water bottles were lined up on the bleacher seats, and the gym quieted. The terrified energy that had brought everyone to the gym eased. Holly had fallen asleep with her head in Sophia's lap. Erin was across the gym, talking to some of the girls on her soccer team. Mikki stretched out on one of the cots, trying to remember, with the time change, just how long she'd been awake today. The hours in O'Hare were eons ago. Just as she felt herself falling asleep, she heard Erin beside her. "Mikki, there's a piano over there."

Mikki sat up. "What?"

"I said there's a piano on that wall over there." She pointed to an ancient upright, a wooden bench in front of it.

"Okay, I see it."

"Would you play something? All this waiting is so boring and, if we had some music, maybe we wouldn't keep thinking about all the bad things that might be happening." She lightly tugged at Mikki's sleeve.

"Do we have to ask someone?"

"No one's going to care. Is your hand all right to play?"

"Probably." In truth she hadn't given it a thought all day.

Erin took Mikki's hand, making sure she would follow. Standing in front of the piano, Mikki tested a few of the keys, ran a quick scale. It didn't look like much but it was at least in tune. Erin looked inside the piano bench. "Hey, there's music in here if you need it."

Mostly sheet music from the thirties and forties. Music that the older people would recognize, maybe they'd even sing along.

Mikki began and, with Erin seated on a folding metal chair, choosing the music, they soon had an audience. Occasionally, someone provided an off-key solo. To one side, a couple was doing a slow two-step to *The Way You Look Tonight*.

When Erin ran out of sheet music, "What else do you know?"

Mikki smiled. "If you get us some water, I'll try something different."

Her own music. By the time Erin returned with the water, Mikki was halfway through the first composition, one that Jay had critiqued and written lyrics for.

She ran through all the pieces she'd turned in to Northwestern, stopping between pieces to massage her hand. It didn't hurt, but she didn't want it to get tight. Some of the original audience wandered away. This music wasn't danceable or sing-able and it was getting late.

Mikki played and played. She felt like she could go on forever. No audience, no applause. Just music. Hers.

Erin eventually gave up and went back to the cots.

As Grace emptied an over-full trash can into the dumpster behind the gym, she tried not to look at the fierce red glow to the south where her greenhouses were. She didn't care what happened to the house, just the plants. Would the jury-rigged sprinkler system on the roofs and around the buildings actually work? It hadn't been tested before. Walking back inside, she pulled her phone from her back pocket and turned it on, wondering when she'd turned if off. She almost never turned it off. Hank's picture came up on the screen. **Mom: SOS.** Trembling she read the rest of his text and hurried inside. She would tell Sophia later; now she needed someone with access to help. She called Manny.

When she had convinced Manny's son to meet her near the stone cairn, Grace appeared beside the piano, pulling Erin's chair alongside the bench. As soon as Mikki realized Grace was there, she stopped playing. "What's going on?"

"I need a partner in crime."

Careful not to wake Sophia or the girls, Mikki retrieved her purse and left the gym. Grace was ahead of her, striding toward the van. The door locks beeped and Mikki climbed into the passenger side, her heart thumping. Whatever was wrong must involve Hank. Not until the van was on Highway 74, heading directly into Evergreen and the fire, did Grace explain.

"I got a text from Hank a couple hours ago, but my phone was off while I was handing out sandwiches. Dante's injured and Hank was asking for help. He sent his location, but now his phone isn't working."

"So what are we going to be able to do?"

"I called Manny. His youngest son Carlo is on paternity leave from his EMT job in Kittridge. He's meeting us near the stone cairn."

Just before they reached the police barricade outside Evergreen, Grace turned onto a narrow street that, in a mile or so, turned into crumbling asphalt, angling through forest that hadn't burned, the angry red/orange glow not all that far away, silhouetting the trees. Even though the van's beams were on high, seeing through the smoke and darkness required Grace to slow down to barely ten miles an hour. She stopped twice to stare at a grouping of trees, then a fence. "I'm not exactly lost, but the smoke changes the look of things."

The road got rougher, skirting the eastern perimeter of the town. Grace seemed unbelievably calm, eyes alertly scanning the road. Mikki, however, was stiff with a fear she'd never experienced before, an aching hollowness. Any shift in the wind and the fire would engulf them. They could die, swiftly and painfully. Dante and Hank might already be dead. Hank's text was two hours old. As unhappy as Mikki had been about her life in the last year, she did not want to die, didn't want anyone to die. Especially not Hank. Though she'd been quick to run off with *Tangerine Slices*, he had become an important part of her life. The non-performing part.

She looked at Grace's determined profile, jaw set, leaning forward, keeping her eyes on the road. Unexpectedly, she braked hard. Even with the seatbelt, Mikki was pulled forward. Before she could push herself back, Grace threw the van into reverse, then made a sharp right.

"What is it?" Mikki was bracing herself against the dashboard, hoping her hand was okay.

"We're close. See that pyramid of stones and the recent tire tracks? Those are probably from Carlo's pick-up. He got here really fast." In another five minutes, Mikki saw Hank's black SUV with its lights directed on a silver pick-up crumpled against a tree. The windshield shattered, the driver's door open.

Grace set the van's brake, turned the engine off, and jogged to where Carlo was kneeling beside one of the figures lying on the bare dirt. Mikki couldn't make herself move. The man that Carlo was helping was Hank, fastening some kind of oxygen mask over Hank's face. Grace was kneeling beside them. When the mask was on, Carlo and Grace helped Hank sit up, then lean against the rear tire on Carlo's truck. He looked like a ghost, ashes and dirt covering him from head to foot. He was at least okay enough for Carlo and Grace to leave him. Mikki felt tears seep onto her cheeks.

Grace was already on her knees beside Dante when Carlo joined her with his medical bag, a folding stretcher, and another oxygen mask. She helped him put the mask on Dante, watched as Carlo examined the head wound, then carefully ran his hands over Dante's torso. He pulled back one of Dante's eyelids, shining a small light into the eye. Turning the light off, he opened his medical bag, pulled out disinfectant, sterile pads, and bandages, then cleaned the wound on Dante's head.

Working up her courage, Mikki left the van, walked over to Hank, paused uncertainly, then sat on the ground beside him and took his hand. At her touch, he straightened a little, looked at her and squeezed her hand. For a few moments, she almost forgot how dangerous their situation was.

Grace's voice reached Mikki, "We need you over here."

Carlo stood. "As we lift him onto the stretcher, hold it still." He showed her where to kneel and place her hands; then he and Grace, an inch at a time, carefully maneuvered Dante's ash-covered body onto the stretcher. To hold it took more strength than Mikki expected.

Once Dante was covered with a light blanket and strapped to the stretcher, Carlo walked over to Grace's van, opened the sliding door on the right side, and looked in. "It'll be easier for us to lift him into your van; it's lower and covered."

Grace expertly positioned her van parallel to the stretcher. Then, with Grace at Dante's feet and Carlo at his head and shoulders, they lifted the stretcher into the delivery van. "Mikki, I need you to sit beside him, steady him as much as you can. Grace, once I get Hank into my truck, follow me. I'm going back to Kittridge and then figure out which hospital to take them to. We need to get out of here. The wind's picking up."

He took out his phone, tapped several times, and waited. "This is Carlo Aguilar, Kittridge Ambulance. I have two men injured in the fire. One critical, the other ambulatory. Both with smoke-inhalation and other injuries. Coming from Evergreen." He listened. Then slid his phone into his pocket. "They'll get back to me."

A few minutes later, he pulled alongside the van and shouted, "All right ladies, let's roll."

Grace started the engine and looked back at Mikki. "Find something to hang onto."

In a *déjà vu* moment, it occurred to Mikki that the last time she'd held onto something in a vehicle, her world fell apart.

While he was lying on the ground beside Dante, Hank had been pretty sure they were going to die. Realistically, chasing Dante into a wildfire was a fool's errand, except Hank wasn't a fool; he was a doctor who'd taken the Hippocratic oath to save lives. This might classify as an attempt to save a life. There wasn't, however, anything in that oath that said he had to give up his own life. He'd rolled onto his stomach, his arms folded to hold his face off the ground so he wouldn't inhale as much smoke.

How long he lay there, Hank had no idea. He was slipping in and out of consciousness. Not sure whether he was dreaming, he heard his mother talking to a male voice. An oxygen mask was being fitted over his nose and mouth, his pulse being checked. The male voice asked him if he could hear him. Hank nodded.

Moments passed. He was leaning against a truck tire. In a few more minutes, someone took his hand; he turned to find Mikki sitting beside him. Hoping he wasn't hallucinating, he squeezed her hand. She definitely felt very real. She'd come to help him. He smiled into the mask.

At the gym, Sophia had pushed two cots together so Erin and Holly could be close together. Though the girls had been wound up with fear, they fell asleep as soon as they lay down. Satisfied that she could relax a little, Sophia slept too.

It was nearly 3 a.m. when one of the Red Cross workers gently shook her shoulder. "Are you Sophia Perillo?"

In the darkened gym, Sophia struggled to see the person who was talking to her. "Yes." She pushed herself to a sitting position.

"Do you have your phone?"

"Someplace."

"There's a text message on it about your husband. A woman named Grace asked me to tell you."

Sophia fumbled in her purse for her phone, "Thank you." Standing up, she walked outside so she wouldn't disturb anyone. She was trembling as she opened the message app: **Call me. Grace**

Sophia found Grace's cell number and hit it. Grace answered immediately. "They're alive."

Relief sucked the air from Sophia's lungs.

"Sophia, did you hear me?"

She gasped, "Yes."

"We're at Kindred. Put it into your GPS. I have no idea how we got here. I just followed Carlo. When you check out of the evacuation center, check Mikki and me out too. We left without doing that. I know they keep a head count."

It took almost half an hour to get Erin and Holly sorted. As soon as Sophia pulled onto I-70, the girls were back asleep. She forced herself to concentrate on the GPS voice that was telling her where to go. She didn't dare go back to sleep. Fortunately there was almost no traffic.

Dante was alive. That was all that mattered, not the house or the workshop. The image of him attempting to hold off the fire with the garden hose had been both ludicrous and terrifying.

Since she wasn't next of kin to either Dante or Hank, Mikki let Grace and Carlo deal with the checking in process, pulled a chair close to the waiting room wall, and leaned against it. She was asleep in seconds. All the way into Denver, she'd intently watched Dante, steadied him and herself and the stretcher whenever the van turned. He was so pale. What if he died while she was taking care of him? She'd never before been responsible for another human being.

After delivering his two patients to the emergency room, Carlo called his father while he was driving toward Kittridge. "I'm heading back home. Sonia needs to get to work. I'm on baby duty."

"How's Hank?"

"Smoke inhalation, a few cuts and bruises. The other guy is in much worse shape. He hasn't regained consciousness. They're doing tests. Probably ribs, concussion, can't tell till they do an MRI. He really did a number on himself and his truck."

"Thanks son. Kiss the grandbaby."

"Copy that."

On day two of the *Evans* fire, dingy orange smoke dimmed the morning sun. As soon as they were cleared to fly, two helicopters began dipping water from Echo Lake, and a fixed wing plane filled with retardant began attacking the forward line of the fire, giving the overnight ground crews some relief. The wind was lighter, the humidity higher than yesterday. At least eleven structures had been destroyed, countless others damaged. The central part of Evergreen was untouched, but the evacuation order was still in effect. It was too early to send people back home.

It was going to be another long day. At the evacuation center, the Red Cross began setting up for breakfast.

Just before noon, needing to see what had happened to the greenhouses, Manny risked going into the burn area. Both sides of the road leading to Grace's property were charred, glowing spots still deciding whether to go out or reignite. When he pulled onto Grace's property, he stopped his truck and sat there in awe. The greenhouses, with their Rube Goldberg sprinkler systems, were untouched. Grace's frame house, however, had burned to the ground, some of the debris floating in the swimming pool. Before he got caught in the fire zone, he reversed out of the driveway and drove back the way he'd come. He wouldn't call Grace just yet. She had enough on her plate with Hank. As soon as the evacuation was lifted, he'd get into the greenhouses to evaluate the condition of the plants.

In the midst of a dream that involved skiing, Mikki heard Holly's voice: "Wake up, Aunt Mikki."

She resisted until she heard Sophia's voice and opened her eyes reluctantly.

Sophia, usually well turned out, was disheveled, looking like she needed sleep and a change of clothes. "Can you take the girls to Greeley in my car? They don't need to stay here. And maybe you could convince Grace to go with you. She looks like she's going to fall over."

"Can I see Hank?"

"No. For today, they have him in the ICU. You're not a relative and Erin's too young to go in." She handed Mikki the car keys.

With effort, Mikki stood up. "Where is she?"

Grace was seated across from the nurses' station on the second floor. Mikki took the seat next to her. "How is he?"

"Stable. They only put him up here so they can keep a close check on his breathing. They'll move him to a regular room later today. He's sleeping."

"Sophia thinks you should come to Greeley with me and the girls. Get a shower, eat real food—well, take out—and if anything changes, I can bring you back."

The fact that Grace docilely agreed to go to Greeley with Mikki showed she'd reached the end of her rope. By default, Mikki was in charge of food, showers, and sleeping arrangements for various people.

A first.

As soon as they arrived, Mikki ordered pizzas and salads, which were quickly devoured. Grace took up residence in the master bedroom; the girls were in the guest room, wearing Jon's t-shirts as nightgowns. By eight o'clock, everyone except Mikki was in bed. An hour later, Sophia texted that there was no new information about the patients, so Mikki showered, found her pj's, and curled up on the couch, not the most comfortable spot, her phone on the floor in easy reach. She was dead to the world within five minutes.

No one in the Greeley house moved until eleven. Grace woke first, brewed coffee, and called Sophia's cell. Then called Manny. By the time Mikki wandered into the kitchen, Grace had a yellow lined pad in front of her, making a list.

"Have you heard from Sophia?"

"I called her half an hour ago. Dante's still unconscious, but the MRI didn't pick up any problem. She sounds awful."

"What about Hank?"

According to one of the nurses on his floor, he thinks they should discharge him. Doctors make terrible patients. But they're keeping him another day. Might even send him to rehab for a few days. He will not be pleased."

So relieved he was better, Mikki set about fixing breakfast, the usual cold cereal and milk. There was only one banana, so she saved it for the girls. If any or all of them were back here tonight, grocery shopping would be a must.

"What's the list for?"

Grace laid the pen down. "My house is gone."

"Oh no." Mikki stopped eating. "How did you find out?"

"Manny went to my place yesterday. Fortunately, the greenhouses are okay. He's probably already back there, checking on the plants. The heat may have cooked everything inside."

"I'm so sorry."

"The list is the phone calls I have to make, especially to the insurance company. I doubt the florists in Evergreen are open, but I need to touch base. All my important papers are in the van at the hospital, so Sophia's coming here with the van. She'll pick up her car and go back. I'm meeting up with Manny later. The TV says the fire is moving south, away from Evergreen. It's 45% contained."

"Any news about Sophia's place?"

Grace shook her head. "I'll try to find out. If you want to retrieve your car, I can drop you and the girls at the evacuation center. Assuming I can get into Evergreen, I'll stay at Hank's tonight."

By the time Sophia got to Greeley, the girls were eating breakfast—a little cranky, begging to see their fathers. Sophia shut the conversation down with "Holly, the hospital doesn't allow children in the ICU. Erin, your dad is okay so why don't you keep Holly company today."

With the kids tamped down, she took a quick shower, changed clothes, and headed back to Kindred before Grace, Mikki, and the girls left for Evergreen. Mikki hugged her, but they didn't talk. Talking would tap into emotions neither was ready for.

Though Grace knew what she would see when she pulled into her driveway, actually seeing her house burned to the ground—only parts of the foundation and chimney visible—was gut-wrenching. She leaned her forehead on the steering wheel and struggled for control. Crying was a waste of time—so was anger.

When Manny tapped on the driver-side window, she lowered the glass.

"You okay?"

She sat up. "Jury's out." She opened her door and stepped into the ash/dirt mixture that covered her driveway.

"How're the plants?"

"Better than you might think. I've started disposing of the ones that definitely won't revive. If you're up for it, let's try watering the others a little. Coax them back to life."

Grateful for Manny's steadiness, she nodded. Activity was always better than wallowing.

Sophia was allowed to sit beside Dante until the doctor arrived on his afternoon rounds. Instead of waiting in the hallway, she went looking for Hank's room.

He was sitting up, an oxygen tube in his nose, reading a newspaper. She paused at the door, "Are you allowed company?"

"Yes. You're my first visitor. My mother and Manny are giving CPR to her plants, my daughter is wandering around with your daughter and sister. But you know that. Have you had any sleep?"

"A little. I probably shouldn't be driving though."

"How's Dante? I keep asking the nurses but not getting answers."

She shook her head a little, tears threatening. "Still out."

"What did the scans show?"

"Nothing that explains his not waking up yet."

He held out his hand and she grabbed it. "Thank you for rescuing him."

Hank smiled. "I mostly called for help. Manny's son and my mother did the rescuing. I had to be rescued too."

The last time Grace experienced such a devastating week was when her husband died. The week of the fire, no one died but it was crushing in other ways. While waiting for the overworked insurance adjuster to show up, she and Manny sorted through the plants, disposing of about a third of her stock. Not as bad as it could have been. She ordered replacements from the wholesalers in Colorado Springs, but it would be two or three weeks before they could deliver.

Three days after she returned to Evergreen, she drove to the rehab facility in Denver to collect Hank. Though he had not been a patient patient, his color was back to normal, he didn't need oxygen, and checkups could be done with Nate Price, the Clinic's GP. No working for a few weeks, but Grace suspected he'd figure out a way around that order.

Before she took him to his house, he wanted to see what her place looked like. Sitting in the van, "I can't believe your greenhouses survived."

"The sprinklers were Manny's idea. I should have let him do the house. Since rebuilding my house will take many months, I'm renting a trailer, which should be here day after tomorrow. When Cate comes home, your house will be full, and I need to be out here."

"How big is the trailer?"

"Twenty-eight feet. Since I'm hoping renting it falls under my insurance coverage, I'm getting something called the Flying Cloud. It has a queen-sized bed."

"The girls will be pleased that the pool survived."

She looked at the muck and debris floating on it. "That's low on the clean up list. What about your car?"

"Scorched. Whenever I'm cleared to drive, I'll get a rental until the insurance pays up. I really liked that SUV."

Grace started the van and backed into the road. "Now that Dante's awake and responding to treatment, Sophia doesn't need to be at the hospital as much, so she's coming up tomorrow to look at their place. According to Manny, the workshop is a total loss, but only part of their house is damaged."

"So Sophia and Holly will stay in Greeley a while longer?"

"Yes. Jon and Ardith returned yesterday. I'll bring Erin up in a couple of days. Sophia will stay there as long as Dante's in the hospital and then in rehab. Not sure what the plan is for Holly when school opens. You may end up with three kids. The girls don't want to miss their first days at Evergreen Middle. They're already planning what to wear."

As she pulled into Hank's driveway, "Even though you haven't asked, I suspect you're curious about Mikki." She didn't wait for a response. "She's rented an apartment in Arvada and is sleeping on an air mattress until her furniture comes from Chicago. A week or so."

Hank wasn't surprised that Grace had read his mind. She was annoyingly good at seeing right through him, and she probably knew Mikki hadn't visited him in the hospital or rehab. Knowing his mother, she was curious about that.

Seeing the southern edge of Evergreen for the first time was a shock. The firefighters had managed to save many of the structures, but the trees were charred sticks, the ground cover gone. A ghost forest. It would be years before the scars would disappear. His house, like most of the structures in town, wore a thick film of ash. They needed a good rain to help clean it off. A minor issue, however. The girls were okay, he was almost okay, Cate would be home soon, and Mikki had rented an apartment within driving distance.

Don't get ahead of yourself, Duncan.

Dante had been awake for several days, though he was still struggling to recall the events that put him in the hospital with a concussion, as well as a broken shoulder and collarbone. In lieu of a cast that would have awkwardly elevated his arm, making everything difficult, his arm was strapped to his chest. He was still on oxygen, and there was discussion about his going to rehab as soon as the concussion improved.

Sophia came everyday. Since the oxygen mask interfered with their ability to communicate, she brought him a pad and pen.

Our place?

"I'm going up tomorrow. I have an appointment with the insurance adjuster. We'll know more then."

Holly?

"She's with Dad and Ardith until school starts. I'll bring her when you're approved for visitors."

With his right hand, he gave her a one thumb up. She smiled and settled herself in the chair by the window. She'd downloaded a book on her Kindle, but concentrating was hard when there were so many bits and pieces of their life to sort out. The Symphony had brought in a substitute for her position; next week, she was due to return to finish out the summer performances.

Holly was happily spending time with Jon and Ardith, but Ardith would be back to work the first week of August. Jon would be back at the University a week later. She needed to ask Hank if Holly could stay with him once school started. The fire had effectively undone almost everything in their lives. And even if there were something left of the workshop, Dante wouldn't be able to work for months. During and after the fire, she'd been afraid for Dante; now she was afraid to see the house and workshop by herself, so she asked Mikki to go with her to meet the adjuster.

Because of the chaos following the fire, Mikki hadn't had time to over-think the ramifications of renting herself a place somewhere in the

Denver metro area. The apartment complex in Arvada had been built in the seventies. Not all that elegant, but functional and not too pricey. She had a two-bedroom, first floor apartment at the back of the complex. She'd made it clear to the manager that she would be renting a piano for the second bedroom and, yes, there would be practicing. Thankfully, he gave her the green light. The piano was due in a few days. It had been way too long since she'd been able to practice.

The contents of her storage unit in Chicago were already headed for Denver. In the meantime she was using some of Ardith's camping gear. The utilities had been turned on and her mail was being forwarded from Greeley. She'd changed addresses so often in the last two years that the Post Office would probably appreciate her staying in one place for a while.

The first night in the apartment, she got a text from Noah, who had been silent for the last month. **Baby Boy Stein, 7lbs. 10 ozs. born August 2nd. Nicholas Jay. All ok, Love**

OMG. You're a father. I love the name. Send a picture. Love M

Sophia told Mikki she'd pick her up around ten. "I want to see your apartment."

Mikki couldn't refuse Sophia's request to go to Evergreen with her. For once, her sister needed her.

They hugged at the apartment door; then Sophia stepped inside and surveyed the empty living room. "I love what you've done with the place."

Mikki laughed. "How do you really feel?"

"Sorry. You at least have four walls and a roof. I may not have any of those."

Sophia had promised herself not to cry when she saw the house, but she couldn't stop the tears from seeping onto her cheeks. Dante's workshop was rubble; all the wood inside had furnished additional fuel for the wildfire. It looked like a bomb had been dropped on it. The firefighters had undoubtedly put their efforts into saving the house. It was brick and the roof metal, but the fire had crept inside via the wooden eaves. Telling Dante about the workshop and house would be incredibly hard.

In what was left of the Perillo driveway, the sisters sat in the car, looking at the house. Mikki was holding Sophia's hand. "Can we go inside?"

"It might not be safe. Maybe we can look in the windows."

Mikki let go of Sophia's hand and opened the car door.

The wing with Holly's bedroom and the guest room was pretty much gutted, the living/dining room too. The kitchen looked like it had serious water damage, but the other wing with the soundproof studio was in much better condition. "Might know, Mom's piano survived."

Mikki surveyed the debris scattered across the yard. Most of the trees would have to be removed. "Do you think Dante will rebuild the workshop?"

Sophia shrugged, unwilling to revisit the problems with Dante and his work.

"He has a long healing process ahead." *Psychologically and physically.* The meeting with the marriage counselor seemed eons ago.

They retreated to the car to wait for the adjuster.

The rental piano, a spinet with an above average sounding board, was delivered on schedule. Mikki was so delighted that she practiced too long and too hard; as a result, her hand tightened up for the first time in a month. A brief rest was needed. Her furniture arrived a few days later and, though the movers placed the furniture for her, there were a dozen boxes of books, bedding, and kitchen equipment to sort through. She was arranging the kitchen cupboards when Grace called for a favor.

"I promised to take Erin home tomorrow, but I finally have a contractor coming to give me an estimate on rebuilding—well there's no re—just building my house. Could you deliver her to Hank?"

A no-brainer. Grace had not only saved Hank's life but also done all sorts of necessary tasks for everyone during and after the fire. "Of course."

However, going to Hank's meant she'd have to talk to Hank, at least briefly. That was making her just a little uneasy. Other than holding his hand the night of the fire, they'd had no contact since the night of the concert at Red Rocks.

That was May. This was August.

Was it over? Did she want it to be over? She missed his company, the sex, the weekends at Greeley. She'd shared herself with him in ways she'd never done with another man. Until now, their relationship had moved forward because he moved it. She was the one who kept leaving town, trying to resurrect a lifestyle that didn't want to be resurrected. Perhaps he was tired of doing all the moving.

During the trip into the mountains, Erin's non-stop monologue didn't require Mikki to participate beyond one or two words at appropriate intervals. No question, Erin was excited to finally be going home. When Mikki turned onto Hank's street, Erin squealed. "It looks the same. It looks the same." After seeing Sophia's, Mikki was also relieved, just not squealing.

Erin was out of the car, racing into the house before Mikki released her seat belt. She stayed put, giving Hank and Erin private time. After a few minutes, she rolled Erin's suitcase onto the porch, returned to get the small backpack and her own purse—then sat on the top step and waited.

The screen door opened. "You can come in, you know."

Mikki stood, "Just giving Erin time with you."

Now he was on the porch, standing beside her. "Hi."

"Hi."

Terrible dialogue.

His eyes held her. No actual touching. But she felt like he was touching her. He looked—like Hank, wearing the same cargo shorts and t-shirt he'd worn at Erin's birthday party last year. She wanted him to touch her. To wrap his arms around her and tell her he'd missed her.

"Come to the kitchen. I'll deal with Erin's stuff later. She's in her room talking to Holly, telling her about our house, about Evergreen. They've only been separated for part of an afternoon. Talk about joined at the hip. Instead of coffee, I made iced tea. Too warm for coffee."

In the kitchen, they sat at the round kitchen table. "You look okay."

"Mostly I am. I'm cleared to drive; now I'm shopping for a car. Cate will pitch a fit if she can't enjoy her shiny new driver's license."

"When does she arrive?"

"Two days. Mom is meeting her. Finally, all of us under the same roof." He paused, "I hear you have a roof of your own."

Nice seque. "I do."

The conversation stalled. Fortunately, Erin broke the awkwardness, "Hol says her dad's getting out of rehab soon. Where's my stuff?"

"Outside." He went to the porch, then took the suitcase and backpack to her room.

Back in the kitchen, "More tea?"

"No thanks."

He refilled his glass and sat down. "Do you like your apartment?"

"I guess so. It keeps me from moving into other people's homes. The best part is having the rental piano and my furniture. I even have a parking space." *The world of ordinary.* "So when do you go back to work?"

"On Tuesday. My schedule's going to be light. When you're off the grid for a while, patients find other places to get better."

"Sophia says your mother likes living in the trailer."

"My mother has a backbone of steel and more energy than others half her age. She likes the trailer because it doesn't require much upkeep. She's never been one for housework."

"She made your rescue happen."

"Yes she did. How did she recruit you?"

"She asked me to go with her and didn't explain what she had in mind until we were in the van. I wasn't much help."

Softly, "You held my hand."

The way he said it caught her unawares. Hearts did skip beats.

She nodded. Not trusting her voice.

"You didn't come to see me in the hospital."

"Sorry."

"Why?"

"I didn't know whether—after I went off with the band—" She suddenly felt shy. He was almost smiling. "We were sleeping together."

"Yes."

He moved his glass to one side, intent. "I wish you'd visited. Did you think about visiting?"

She took a deep breath. "Yes."

"But—"

"You have a life that fits you."

"It would fit better if it included you."

"I'm not good at being part of—maybe anything except a band and my own family. They've had to put up with my gypsy ways a long time. Noah just became a father."

Hank laughed.

"What so funny? The baby's middle name is Jay."

"It's the non sequiturs."

"The ideas are related. Noah and I were gypsies together for a long time, and now he's not a gypsy."

"Oh."

"And—I'm still sort of a gypsy. By myself."

"Do gypsies have apartments?"

"Don't make fun."

"I'm not. Maybe you aren't as gypsy as you think you are."

She shrugged. "I should get on the road. Thanks for the tea. I'm glad you're doing well."

He followed her to her car, opened the door for her. "Thanks for delivering Erin."

"No problem."

"Don't be a stranger." He kissed her lips gently and, before she could respond, moved away. "Safe trip."

Because Sophia couldn't be in two places at once—rehearsing with the Symphony and taking Dante to Greeley—she asked Mikki to fill in for her. "This should be the last time I need you to do the Uber thing."

"No worry. What's the address?"

All of them had been shuffling people and cars since the fire. Now that Hank had transportation, moving the girls around was easier. During the week, they were in Evergreen in school. On weekends, Jon brought Holly to Greeley to be with her mother and visit her father in rehab.

Cate was home, trying to impress everyone with *When I was living in New York*. She was already online, downloading college applications. Hank wanted her to stay in Colorado; Cate however had her heart set on an East Coast school. The out-of-state tuition costs were seriously interfering with his sleep.

When Mikki arrived at the rehab facility, Dante was sitting in the lobby, his left arm still strapped to his chest. Otherwise, he looked pretty much like he always had, the wound on his forehead already scabbed over. One of the male nurses loaded his suitcase and several plastic bags with books and toiletries into Mikki's car, making sure Dante was comfortably settled in the passenger seat. Waving as they drove away.

Other than asking about her apartment, Dante was silent until they were close to Jon and Ardith's.

"Can we park someplace for a few minutes?"

Puzzled, Mikki turned into the Safeway lot and shut the engine off.

"Before I have to confront the real world, I want to ask you about having your life turned upside down. About your hand. Losing what you worked so hard for. How do you cope? I feel like I'm in a similar place. Sort of lost."

Not what Mikki expected.

Not what she wanted to talk about.

"I'm not sure I'm coping all that well. It's almost a year and a half, and I'm still unemployed."

"You're back in Denver with a place of your own."

"That's about the only thing I do have, and I have that only because I can't continue moving in with friends and family. I'm wearing out my welcome pretty much everywhere."

He was quiet for several minutes. Then, "The family counselor Soph and I met with before the fire told me something I hadn't anticipated," he hesitated, "that the workshop, my business, was running me instead of me running it. He wondered if I had ever thought of using my love of working with wood some other way. Since I've been laid up, I keep going back to that idea. Even though Sophia hasn't described what the workshop looks like, I know it's gone. It was burning when I left our driveway. The fire has taken my life's work without my permission. Like a no-choice change. Same with you and the bus crash."

Mikki took a minute. "I keep trying to give my career CPR. Biding my time until I miraculously get it all back. So far, no miracle. Your counselor may have a point—at least for you."

"Isn't there some other way to be a musician?"

Reluctantly, "I guess."

"Have you tried any other way?"

"Only making up the units I needed to finish my degree. I did an Independent Study using some of my compositions."

"Is there a way you can have them performed?"

Mikki smiled. "You do realize you're the one giving me advice."

Sheepishly, "Yeah."

"What advice are you giving yourself?"

"Since we'll probably be living at Jon's until our house is habitable, I'm going to do what I swore I'd never do, work at my father's store. He wants me to redesign his showroom—it's looked the same for twenty plus years. I'd be a design advisor. Maybe modernize his inventory. It's a one-time thing. No heavy lifting required."

"I thought you hated the idea of selling."

"I still do. This isn't actual selling. And we need the money."

They sat in the parking lot a while longer. Then Mikki started the car, "Maybe we should get to Dad's; they'll wonder what's taking so long,"

By Labor Day, the fire was 90 % contained and people whose homes weren't damaged were doing massive amounts of clean-up. A sense of normalcy was returning.

Each weekday morning, Hank set out three cereal bowls. The girls had begged to buy lunch in the cafeteria, so no packed lunches. Cate was allowed to drive Erin and Holly to the middle school, drive herself to the high school, and park Hank's new SUV in the school lot. She liked the responsibility. Being a senior with a driver's license was doing wonders for her attitude. If however there was soccer practice in the afternoon, she also had to take them and pick them up, effectively freeing Grace and Hank's schedules. Since running in the morning was not yet allowed, the walk to and from the Clinic served as Hank's exercise.

Now that she'd chosen a contractor and the insurance company was getting closer to settling her claim, Grace was in the process of designing what her new house would look like, what features to include to make her life easier. She already knew she was going to have a gas-fueled fireplace. Splitting kindling and building fires had long ago lost their charm. Actual construction might not get started until spring, given Colorado's frequent winter snowstorms. Fortunately, Duncan Gardens was back in business, so she didn't spend all that much time in the trailer anyway.

Sophia and Dante's house was almost ready for camping out. The living/dining room and the wing with Holly's room and the guest room were still a mess, the kitchen usable but not finished. The studio and master bedroom were serving as sleeping and living quarters. At least the house had a new roof; the electricity and water were back on. Because Dante didn't yet have full use of his shoulder and arm, he wasn't driving. On the days Sophia had to be in Denver, she dropped him off at his father's store. Otherwise, he was working from home.

As soon as there was less to-ing and fro-ing, Mikki retreated to her apartment. Practicing and thinking. She had a possible plan, which she was keeping to herself. She wasn't sure she liked the plan or that it could work. It had taken her several days to put together a resume, something she'd never done before.

Since Noah was sending her weekly photos of the baby, she sent him the rough draft of the resume for his input. He suggested a couple of ideas, asking, *"Where's it going?"*

"Sorry, it's still a plan in progress."

His return message, which contained several emojis making rude gestures, made her laugh.

Mikki sent the resume along with letters from two Northwestern faculty members and a recording of three of her compositions to all the community colleges and universities in the area. Then waited.

And waited.

Making contact via snail mail was definitely not working, so she gathered her courage and made appointments by phone with the Deans of three music departments. Putting herself out there was not her style, but she needed some kind of work. In early October, she got a call from Denver Community offering a meeting with the chairperson of the music program. They were looking for someone to tutor piano students who were struggling but couldn't afford private instruction. The department had recently received a grant that would cover ten hours of tutoring a week. Since it was already the halfway point of the Fall term, she'd essentially be rescuing students in jeopardy of failing their piano requirement. Five students had been identified as needing support. She'd meet with them on Tuesdays and Thursdays, an hour each day.

Tutoring sounded a lot like teaching, but Mikki wasn't in a position to be picky. She accepted.

As the interview ended, Matt Greenbriar, who was in charge of the grant, suggested she might look into getting a master's degree, the standard requirement for teaching at the community college level. "You have unique experience; you just need the paper if you want to move into education."

In truth, she wasn't sure she wanted to.

The tutoring income, admittedly small, would cover some of her day-to-day expenses, like food and gas. Rent and everything else would have to come out of the money she'd made with *Tangerine Slices*. She might get by until next summer. No guarantees.

The first Tuesday she met with the students, she evaluated their playing, then reported to their individual instructors online what her recommendations were. Her first student, Elena, was in her second year, studying voice. The piano class was a graduation requirement. She arrived sulky and defensive. Being sent for tutoring was clearly hurting her pride. She had long dark hair pulled into a ponytail and was wearing jeans, a short sleeved sweater, and flip-flops. Mikki took note of the flip-flops. Also noted were the elaborate tattoos on her arms. Not a thing Mikki was going to do about those, but the flip-flops needed to go. Elena's playing was, in a word, sloppy. When a passage was too difficult, she skipped a chord or a run and kept going, as though those passages weren't necessary.

Mikki could suddenly hear her mother: *Until you can play ALL the notes correctly, slow down. Once you know what the notes are, the speed will come.* OMG, she was channeling her mother. She wanted to call Sophia to share the irony. But since no one in her family knew what she was attempting, there would be no sharing yet. If she failed, she didn't need to advertise.

Jordan was the second student, then Melanie, Terance, and Cliff. Each had some basic problems that, in Mikki's view, should have been addressed long before now. Except for Cliff, they had all been taking lessons in some form since high school. Because she only had seven weeks to get them up to speed, she spent Wednesday afternoon on campus, getting the department secretary to run copies of their sheet music for her.

Not everything could be solved at once. First things first. Prepare them for the performance. The problem for Mikki was how to make that happen. She knew how to make her own hands create music, but how did she get someone else's hands to do what she did instinctively. Once she had the sheet music, she played and replayed everything, noting possible trouble spots. On her phone, she recorded her renditions of each piece. When all else failed, they could hear how a passage should sound.

After five difficult sessions on Thursday, Mikki called her sister. She needed input. They scheduled breakfast at a coffee shop a block from Boettcher Hall because Sophia had a ten o'clock call for the Symphony. Mikki was already seated, scanning a menu, when Sophia arrived.

Mikki stood to hug her. "You look better than the last time we were together."

Sophia slipped out of her jacket and laid it on the seat next to her. "Thanks to more sleep, fewer trips up and down the mountain, and less trauma. Still lots of problems to untangle."

"How's Dante?"

"Amazingly good. We're good, well, better. Since we're living in two rooms and a kitchen, we need to be good. No place to hide. Are you going to attend Holly's birthday party next Sunday?"

"Since I was AWOL for her promotion ceremony in June, I promised her. Are you still going to Arrowhead Park?"

"I'm hoping the weather cooperates. If it rains or snows, Hank said we could use his house."

Hank.

"So, what do you want to talk about?"

"Teaching piano."

"Teaching? You? Really?" She was sincerely shocked.

Before Mikki could reply, the waitress came to take their orders, giving Mikki extra breathing time before revealing her new job. "Have you ever tried to teach someone to play the violin? Or the piano?"

"To a total beginner?"

"Let's say intermediate. A twenty year old."

"So polishing and correcting, no scales or Bach Etudes."

"I guess that's a good description."

"No, I haven't. But I remember when Mom was giving me lessons, she would drill and drill on whatever I was doing badly and leave the other stuff alone. Mostly it worked. And when it didn't, it was back to drills. Jeez, she was tough. Why the question?"

Mikki steadied herself and explained.

And as usual, Sophia complained that Mikki hadn't told anyone what she was doing.

"Don't go there, Soph. I need ideas."

"Have you given up on performing?"

"Performing has given up on me."

While they ate, they brainstormed ideas. No big solutions emerged, but talking about learning and teaching in general helped Mikki give form to what she needed to do.

Sunday morning, Cate offered to take Erin to Arrowhead Park for Holly's party, any excuse to drive Hank's SUV.

"No thanks. I have to go to Home Depot, so I'll take her."

Cate leaned against the kitchen counter, smiling. "I don't suppose your errand has anything to do with Mikki being at the party." His daughter had returned from New York more grown up and more in-your-face, like her mother.

He smiled. Not replying because he might get cornered. And yes, he hoped he'd get a chance to talk to Mikki. Since he'd recovered and Mikki was now living in Denver, he'd been trying to decide the best way to connect with her again. Holly's party was the first opportunity he'd come up with. Having endlessly replayed the night of the fire, Mikki sitting on the sooty ground holding his hand, he had vowed to try one more time to restart their affair. He was pushing forty, had been divorced almost nine years. Too long to be alone. Having children in the house did not keep him from being alone.

Holly's party began at one. Hank drove into the Arrowhead parking area a few minutes early. Erin told him goodbye, grabbed Holly's present, and raced toward the marquee tent covering the picnic tables. He surveyed the lot. Mikki's car wasn't there. A good thing. "Accidentally" meeting her as the party was ending might be easier. He headed to Home Depot.

As parents arrived to pick up Holly's guests, the sky was darkening, the wind battering the rented marquee. Late afternoon rain was in the forecast. Holly and Dante were loading the presents and leftover food into Sophia's car. Sophia, Erin and Mikki were pulling the poles out of the tent, fighting the wind. When Hank arrived, they were about to lose the battle. He hurried to help wrestle the poles out and, once the cloth was on the ground, they started rolling everything together, stuffing it into Sophia's car. "We can do a better job getting everything put together once we're out of the wind."

As fat drops splattered on them, they hurried to the cars. Erin climbed into Hank's SUV while Hank slipped into Mikki's passenger seat. Startled, "Are you in the wrong car?"

"Nope."

The car suddenly seemed too small and definitely too warm. "Do you have to get back to Denver in a hurry?"

"No."

"Would you like to come to dinner at my house? Cate's making spaghetti. There'll be plenty."

An evening with him and his children at his house. They hadn't done anything like that before.

"Yeah, I would."

For a moment she thought he was going to touch her arm, but he opened the car door. "Good. See you at the house."

As he walked away, it occurred to her that it was a good thing the girls would be there. She stayed in the parking lot after the other cars were gone, contemplating the implications of having dinner with him and his daughters. Erin was no problem. They'd spent plenty of time together during the fire. But Cate was an unknown. Ready to go to college, strong-willed. And she could cook a dinner. Not something Mikki would do particularly well.

She started the engine and drove to Hank's.

With Erin's enthusiastic help, Hank built a fire while dinner was cooking, then brought wine for Mikki, hot chocolate for Erin, and a beer for himself.

Erin was recounting the highlights of the party. She and Holly were equally good at monologues. When Cate called her to the kitchen to help, she did not go willingly.

Mikki and Hank were on their own.

The silence stayed until Hank asked, "What are you doing besides moving in and unpacking?"

"Getting rid of things I should never have bothered to put into storage. Learning the neighborhood. And I found my skis."

"Want to go skiing?"

"There's no snow."

"Fair point. Do you have a piano?"

"I'm renting one. To answer your next question, my hand is pretty good. Of course, I'm not performing every night or rehearsing endlessly. So what are you doing besides working and checking up on ex-patients?"

He almost said *waiting for you to figure out where we're going*, but stopped in time.

"Massive amounts of cleaning. There's soot everywhere. Erin said you're tutoring." Ah, the Holly/Erin connection at work. "How are your students doing?"

She shrugged. "Some days they're spot on, some days not. The big question is will they be spot on the afternoon of their recitals."

"Who judges?"

"Five senior faculty members. Pass/fail."

"Tricky."

"Their grades are on the line, probably my job is too."

"Are you looking for other jobs?"

"No."

Good news.

"But Noah is keeping an eye out."

Not good, The Noah factor just wouldn't go away.

"Do you think you'll stay?"

"I don't know."

"If *Tangerine Slices* called, offering you a job, would you go?"

Her knee jerk response was *Yes.*

"What if I asked you to stay?" In for a penny, in for a pound.

"All the time?"

"Let's say most of the time. When you leave, you're gone a long time."

She sat very still, head bent, looking at her hands clasped in her lap, realizing the scars had lost some of their angry redness.

"True."

Softly, "Mikki, look at me."

She did.

"I love you. Do you love me?"

She nodded. "But I don't think I can completely walk away from—my other self. Could you?"

"I already did."

"You're stronger than I am. Less selfish. Sophia always tells me I'm selfish and she's mostly right. Staying would be a huge leap. What if I take the leap and I'm miserable and make you miserable?" She paused, offered a tiny smile. "Grace would hunt me down."

"Undoubtedly. She is a force of nature."

Despite the fact that the girls were in the kitchen, he crossed to where she was sitting and sat beside her, laying his hand against her cheek, intending to kiss her.

"There are children close-by."

He laughed, gently kissed her forehead, and returned to his chair.

Jon and Ardith were hosting the family Thanksgiving. Ardith's brother, his wife, and their fourteen year-old twin daughters were driving from Fort Morgan. Sophia, Dante, Holly and Mikki completed the guest list. Mikki surprised herself by looking forward to being with her family.

There was only one more week of college classes after the holiday weekend. The following week would be various Music Department recitals. Mikki's tutees were scheduled for Tuesday afternoon. She was pretty sure she was more nervous than they were. She'd taken the bull by the horns and outlined what they should wear. "If you want to be taken seriously, you need to look like you take your music seriously." Elena's flip-flops had been banned weeks ago. Hopefully, she would wear long sleeves to hide the tattoos, but that might be asking too much. Mikki recommended nice slacks or skirts. Enclosed shoes. Being the adult for five students made Mikki realize that, at 32, she had changed in unexpected ways. Less flying in the face of convention. Who would have guessed?

Nevertheless, Mikki still didn't trust herself not to go running after an offer to play with a band. The pull of performing was like an addiction with no twelve-step program. She and Hank were seeing one another on weekends. Sometimes they took the girls to the movies, once to a craft fair in Littleton, trying out being a family. Dinner in Evergreen on a few weekends. But no sex, though abstaining wasn't easy for either of them.

The Perillo house was mostly put back together, the rubble that had been the workshop hauled away, the charred trees cut down. Sophia had resigned from her extra job as principal for the violins. "It takes more time than I have right now." From Mikki's view, her sister and Dante seemed to be in a better place.

All of them picking up the pieces, healing a little at a time.

The Wednesday before the recitals, Mikki received a call from Cliff's uncle, Ted Ricco, asking to meet with her over lunch the next day. "I have a job offer for you." No clue about the kind of job or where. She agreed to meet him in a small Mexican restaurant near Larimer Square.

Torn between curious excitement and the fear that she'd have to make a major life decision just when she'd begun to settle into her new life, she didn't sleep much that night.

Fiftyish, handsome, salt and pepper hair, Ted was already seated at a window table in the restaurant. She checked her watch; she'd meant to be early. He stood as she approached the table. "Mikki?" She nodded. "Don't worry, you're not late. I'm early. A habit I can't seem to break."

She sat opposite him, the waitress instantly beside her. "What would you like to drink?"

"Coffee, please."

"Thank you for coming. My nephew sings your praises, says he's learned so much with your tutoring."

"He's worked hard. But he's really nervous about Tuesday's recital. Are you a musician?"

"No. More an appreciator of music. I'm the director of Evergreen's Jazz Festival. Do you know it?"

"My niece and I attended a performance a year ago. In the Lake House."

"One of our best venues."

The waitress returned with the coffee, took their orders, and retreated.

"You said something about a job."

"I did. I've done my research on your career. Very impressive."

"Not so impressive recently."

"The job I have isn't about you performing. There are three divisions in our organization, one of which is education. Arranging workshops for young people, interfacing with the music programs in the local schools, bringing young people into jazz, getting them involved in performing." He paused, "That's been my job for several years. But now I've been promoted, overseeing all three branches, and I need a replacement."

Mikki was surprised. She'd expected the job to be some kind of teaching or performing.

He was waiting for a response. When she didn't say anything, "Does this seem like something you'd be interested in? You certainly have the musical ability. Cliff thinks you're a good teacher. There is, however, a fair amount of management involved."

Mikki took a sip of her coffee, looking for the right thing to say. "I don't have any experience with managing and only these few weeks tutoring. I perform, I compose. That's where my experience has been. I don't know that I'm a good candidate."

"You know the jazz world, have lived in it in a way not many candidates for this job have. To me, that's a plus. You know that side of the business. The other parts you can learn as you go."

He spent the rest of lunch outlining what he had been doing, what was set up for the next year. Explained the make up of the education division, the staff, the timelines. The salary.

So much information. Not the kind of job she'd envisioned for herself—ever.

"What do you think?"

"It's a lot to digest. I've never thought of something like this."

"I understand that playing professionally is very different. But look at it this way: a performance is gone once the performers leave the stage. Its only legacy is a recording. In this job, you're grooming young performers and audiences to love jazz—a long term effect." He took the last bite of his burrito, moved his plate to the side, and reached down for the briefcase on the floor beside his chair. He pulled out a stack of folders.

"Read through our promotional materials. Our office is in the city hall. You're welcome to visit and meet the staff. I'll alert them you might come."

He handed her a business card. "I hope you'll think about the job. I need to move into my new position by the first of next year." He picked up the bill and his briefcase. Still reeling, Mikki had the presence of mind to reach across the table and shake his hand.

"Thanks for the offer. Really, thank you."

"I'd like your answer by the end of December."

Mikki had never been convinced that life events came in clusters of three, until now. The first two were Ted Ricco's job offer and the recitals; then Noah showing up on her doorstep.

She studied the information about the Jazz Festival. Some of the activities were intriguing and, after she paid a visit to the Evergreen offices, she was definitely impressed by the staff. She didn't tell Hank about the offer or her trip to Evergreen. Too soon to put the possibility of the job into the universe. Sophia always thought Mikki's lack of sharing was selfishness or arrogance. But it was more that she was used to following her gut. Other people's input just muddied things.

Layered on top of the job decision was the recital, which only required keeping five young musicians focused during the Tuesday afternoon performances. The event was held in Vanguard Hall, a small venue with a low stage and 250 upholstered seats curved in front of the stage. For the piano recitals, a baby grand was rolled forward from the backstage storage; then the lightweight sliding wall panels were pushed back into place.

The faculty panel was comprised of five music instructors. Three of the judges had to give a pass to each student, based on a ten-minute performance. When Mikki had faced auditions in the past, she'd never been nervous. Today, however, she was a basket case. Elena had actually worn a long-sleeved blouse and nailed her performance. Five passes. Cliff also received five. Terance and Melanie earned four, but Jordan only had two, which meant repeating his class and perhaps being tutored next semester.

Mikki was so proud of them. One of the things she'd always loved about Jay's band was that each musician genuinely appreciated another musician's ability. Mikki hadn't realized that that kind of appreciation could happen in a student/tutor relationship.

Two positive events in the same week.

Her excitement spilled over when she called Hank. "Four out of five isn't bad. I don't think Jordan took the performance as seriously as he should have. I didn't, however, expect him to fail."

"Does this mean you'll be tutoring in the Spring?"

"Don't know. When do the girls take off for Taylor's?"

"Saturday morning. Have you cleared your schedule?" He was taking three vacation days to stay with her. Sex was back in the line up.

"I have."

The girls would spend a week with their mother and fly back on Christmas Eve morning to spend the rest of their break with Hank and Grace.

Event three: Friday night, Noah called from LA. "I'm coming to talk to you. I'll be there early tomorrow morning." No more information.

He was on her doorstep at nine-thirty. Mikki was expecting Hank around eleven. Not a good conjunction of events.

She hugged him, gave him coffee, and admired baby Nick's latest pictures. Finally, "Why are you here?"

"I come bearing gifts." No question that he was pleased with himself. They were sitting across from one another at her industrial-style dining room table. When she'd furnished her Chicago condo, she'd bought what was on the showroom floor whether she liked the style or not. When her furniture arrived in Colorado, she regretted some of her decisions. Especially the table.

Noah grinned, "Guess."

"You know I hate that game. What?"

"I've been designated to offer you the pianist's spot with *Tangerine Slices*. Not filling in. Your job, totally. A contract, the whole works. Rick's leg is giving him no end of trouble. More surgery is scheduled. I begged BG to let me do the honors. However, I have to be on a return flight to LAX this afternoon. No time for celebrating. You'll need to be in LA next week. We're doing a pre-Christmas tour on the West Coast. You already know the music. The office was supposed to send the paperwork to your email this morning."

Mikki reached for her phone and looked at her email. There it was. Her ticket back to the stage. Performing. A good salary. A career reboot.

The miracle was happening.

Why wasn't she more excited? Noah was watching her, expecting her to be thrilled.

But she wasn't. And he noticed.

"What's wrong?"

"It's, well, a surprise. I mean, I've just moved in and—"

"Are you renting or leasing?"

"Renting."

"So give notice, put this stuff in storage. You've done it before."

No argument. But did she want to revisit gypsying?

Until this very moment, she'd been convinced she wanted exactly what he was offering her.

She walked into the kitchen, poured herself more coffee, and brought the pot to refill Noah's cup. Buying time. With a "Yes" she would have her performing life back, restarting her career. Upside down days.

Alone.

Bands weren't forever. Damaged hands probably weren't either.

And she'd be leaving Hank.

Mikki looked into Noah's expectant, smiling face, such a staunch friend through all of this, and said "I don't think I can accept the offer."

"What? You don't want the job?"

Mikki took a deep breath. "No."

"Wow." He sat quietly, not something Noah did often. "I was so sure you'd take the job that I told BG not to go looking for anyone else."

"Six months ago, I probably would have. A lot has happened—changed," she hesitated, "and oddly enough I'm comfortable here, for the time being. Trying out another life."

Noah pulled out his cell phone. "You're sure?"

Mikki nodded.

"Okay. I need to tell BG." His thumbs danced over the tiny keyboard, effectively ending what she'd thought she wanted.

"So what are you going to do instead?"

She hated having to explain herself; she always did it badly, but it was important to make Noah understand. And in the telling, help her understand why she'd declined.

"Career-wise, it's a terrific offer. I'm honored that BG wanted me back. Lightning striking twice. But jobs like this don't last forever."

Somewhat cavalierly, "There'd be another job."

"Maybe. My hand is still an unknown, long term, and I'd be leaving here. At 22, leaving Northwestern to work with Jay was easy, pushing 32 to go back on the road, not so easy. I think I want to be more—anchored."

"You've changed."

Not so much changed as recognizing there were parts of life she'd missed out on.

"In case you haven't noticed, so have you. Husband, father. Come on, that's change."

"Is this about the therapist?"

"Some of it." She hesitated. "I've been offered a job with the Evergreen

Jazz Festival. I'm probably going to take it." She outlined what Ted Ricco had told her.

"A desk jockey. You? I can't imagine it."

"It's different. But I think I need different."

They changed the subject, talked about *Gaining Ground*, reminisced about Jay.

They were standing in the parking lot next to his rental car, hugging goodbye just as Hank's SUV parked in one of the visitor spaces. Noah got in the car and drove away without paying attention to the other vehicle. Once he was out of sight, Hank slowly walked across the parking lot, stopping before he reached her. Keeping his distance.

"When do you leave?" His voice carried anger and sadness. "I'm assuming some sort of job is waiting in the wings."

"Let me—"

"Don't bother to explain. I can't keep waiting for you to circle back when nothing better is in the offing. My heart doesn't do well with uncertainty. I want to be more than a long weekend."

He turned abruptly and was halfway across the lot, his keys in his hand, when she found her voice, "I said no. I didn't take the offer and it was a damned good one too."

Not sure he'd heard correctly, Hank walked back toward her.

"Why not?"

"Do I really have to explain?"

"But you—"

"I want to stay here—with you." At least today she was sure she wanted to.

He returned his keys to his pocket and walked closer. "Are you sure?"

She nodded, feeling joy well up. He looked so dumbstruck, so happy. Because of her. Something about her decision must be right.

She'd explain about the Festival job later—much later.

Printed in the United States
by Baker & Taylor Publisher Services